Grand Canyon Rescue

C. R. Fulton

THE CAMPGROUND KIDS
www.bakkenbooks.com

ISBN 978-1-955657-36-5
For Worldwide Distribution
Printed in the U.S.A.

PUBLISHED BY BAKKEN BOOKS
2022

For everyone who loves solving a clue,
don't forget to use the map
to see if you can discover the answer
*before **The Campground Kids** do!*

The Campground Kids

For more books, check out:
www.bakkenbooks.com

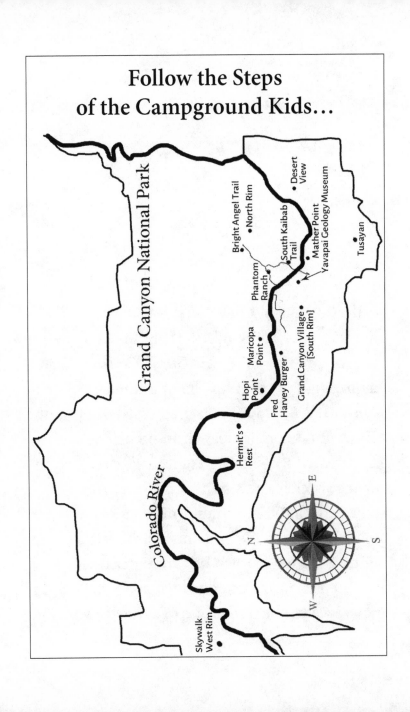

Follow the Steps
of the Campground Kids…

Grand Canyon National Park

Colorado River

Bright Angel Trail
• North Rim

• Desert View

South Kaibab Trail

• Mather Point
Yavapai Geology Museum

• Tusayan

Phantom Ranch

Maricopa Point •

Grand Canyon Village •
[South Rim]

Hopi Point •

Fred Harvey Burger •

Hermit's Rest •

Skywalk West Rim •

-1-

If a 13-year-old boy could ever fly, it would be me, with this hot wind climbing the cliffs before me, rippling my shirt. *The Grand Canyon!* I catch my breath as I see it for the first time. *The Grand Canyon!* With my stomach pressed against the railing and the mile-deep drop-off below, I spread my arms wide. Nothing could have prepared me for the sheer size of this national park!

"Mama, look! It's a California condor!" My ten-year-old sister Sadie exclaims, as she swipes back some of her long brown hair from her face.

I keep my arms extended wide; my fingers tingle as I watch the bird cruise over the canyon.

"It's so wide!" my older cousin Ethan exclaims. *I'm glad he finally has his nose out of the video game he's played the entire way here.*

"Yeah!"

The overlook is crowded. Thankfully, I'm not yet tall enough to block anyone's view, but at 15, Ethan is nearly as tall as my dad. I turn my head when I hear a familiar whistle.

"Dad!" I wave to let him know I see him as he motions us over through the crowds.

"Mom, come on!" I run a hand through my blond hair. The Grand Canyon is hot at the top and even hotter at the bottom, so I'd gotten it cut as short as possible.

Sadie slips up next to me. "It's amazing!" she exclaims as she shakes my elbow.

"Sure is. Hey, got any ideas on why Mom and Dad have been so secretive about this trip?"

"No, but I know they've got something up their sleeves. Have you gotten the name of the campground where we're staying out of them yet?"

"No such luck. Something is going on." I scowl as Mom grins wide when Dad flashes her a quick thumbs up. "See?"

We sidestep a large group and reach Dad.

"I found a great spot for a picture; come on," he says. As he leads us over to some boulders, my heart slams into my toes because the rock just ends. The drop-off seems to last forever. I guess the management of the Grand Canyon doesn't believe in too many railings other than those at the main lookouts.

"Careful!" Dad's wide hand grips my shoulder. "I think that's close enough."

"I'll set up the camera over here." Mom is ready in a few seconds, and we line up in front of one of the seven natural wonders of the world.

While I'm still trying to blink the flash from the camera out of my eyes, Ethan says, "Hey! I bet this boulder would make a funny shot."

Ethan lays down behind it so only his head and hands gripping the rock are showing. And from this angle, it really looks like he's falling into the canyon.

He makes a horrified face, Mom snaps the picture, and then he quips, "What's that?"

"Looks like a…box."

Sadie and I reach for it at the same time.

"Why does it have my name on it?" she asks.

"And mine…" I add. It's a wooden box with strange grooves across it. I take it from Sadie's hand and find it fits in my palm easily. Ethan quickly snatches it from my hand.

"It's got my name on it!" he says happily, as he inspects it.

"Ugh!" Sadie rolls her eyes. "It's got ours too! Let me see it again." Ethan reluctantly hands it over.

I turn to Mom and Dad. "It's from you, right?"

Dad just shrugs, smiling at me.

"It's got to be. No one else in Arizona knows us."

"Isaiah, look! I think it's a puzzle box." Sadie is shifting a section, but it jams against another. I take it from her and start testing the sides.

"Hey, I was working on that!"

I sigh and hand it back. "Let me know when you want help."

Ethan pulls his *Race Tron* game from his back pocket. Soon, his thumbs are flying, and he's leaning around turns that don't exist.

I shake my head then pepper Mom and Dad for details. "What *is* the box for?"

Dad's grin just grows, which propels my already burning curiosity to a higher peak.

"Mom, come on!" I beg, but she simply shrugs.

"Oh! I give up!" Sadie cries.

"Excellent!" I take the box, hungry for answers. Turning it over shows our names are engraved on every side. "*Hmmm.*"

I shift the only piece that's loose, but I can't slide it far before jamming.

"See?" Sadie says, leaning close. "It's stuck."

"Give me a minute." Just when I'm about to admit that she's right, my pinky finger hits a panel on the other side, and the first section shifts farther.

"Oh!" Sadie leans so heavily on my arm I can't continue working.

"Sadie, give me some room, will you?"

"Okay, but hurry! I can't wait to see what's inside!"

I think about the Rubik's Cube I'd received last Christmas. "Maybe if I press here, and twist there…"

-2-

One side of the box slides open an inch. "Almost got it!"

Ethan plops back against the rocks. "*Ugh!* Dead battery? Come on!" He tucks the game into his pocket, unfolds his lanky form, and comes over.

"What's in it?"

All three of us lean close as I convince the panel to slide all the way.

"It's a…" Ethan drops his voice down low, holds his hands high, and throws back his head before announcing, "Nooote!"

I shake my head at his antics, pull out the slip of paper, and hand it to Sadie. She clears her throat and reads: *"Riddle me this, riddle me that, here's a riddle for you..."*

Dear Isaiah, Sadie, and Ethan,

Your mather (or aunt in Ethan's case) pointed out that the best way to keep you out of trouble this trip is to keep you busy. Perhaps with a nice Desert View. Now begins a new adventure, a treasure hunt with a pot of gold you've all been longing for at the end. Follow the mules, I mean clues, but don't expect any help from your mother and me; you've got to figure these out on your own.

Love, Mom and Dad

"Um, Dad, you do realize you misspelled *mother* in the message." I look over at my parents, only to see them whispering and giggling like blissfully happy teenagers.

"*Hmmm,* what? Oh, no help, remember?" Dad says happily.

"Wait…" Sadie says, pointing to the note. "He spelled *mother* correctly the second time…see?"

"Maybe it was on purpose," Ethan takes a guess. "What else is in the box?"

"Nothing." I shake the box, which clunks. "Or maybe something…" I reach in and feel glossy paper. "It's a map of the Grand Canyon National Park!"

Ethan unfolds it.

"Plus…" I dig my finger into the box, feeling a small hole. "…what might be a keyhole!"

"So…" Ethan says, "we've got a keyhole with no key and a note with a misspelled word. Not very much to go on, especially without the help of the lovebirds over there."

"Heard that," Dad says over his shoulder from where he and Mom are holding hands as they enjoy the incredible view.

Sadie adds, "It's a grammatically incorrect note too. He capitalized both Desert and View."

"Plus, he went out of his way to mention mules."

"Wait," Ethan cries, studying the map. "Here's a place called Mather Point!"

Sadie pulls Ethan's arm lower so she can see the map too. "You're right, and there's a campground called Desert View!"

"Yes, but what could the pot of gold be?" I question, tapping my chin.

Sadie chews her lip. "Well, I sure hope we're smart enough to figure it out!"

"Let's head to Desert View first. It's a longer drive, and my game will get charged in the truck by then."

"Seriously, Ethan? Who cares about some game?"

"I do," he says faking hurt.

"Anyway, we can't do that because the first clue is Mather Point, then Desert View, and then the mules. *Eeee!* Do you think we will get to ride mules into the canyon?" Sadie asks.

A smile grows on my face. "I'm up for it."

Mom turns to us. "Do we have a direction yet?"

"Mather Point!" we declare in unison.

"But, Mom, you'll tell us if we're going to the wrong place, right?" I ask.

"Not a chance!" she says joyfully. "Come on!"

Sadie and I frown at each other. "We had better be at the top of our game with Mom and Dad acting so weird."

"Yeah," she agrees.

Mather Point proves well worth the visit. After exploring the Visitor Center where Sadie gathers every available brochure on the park, we take the short trail to the overlook. Somehow this view is even more impressive, and I feel so small gazing out over the depths of the canyon.

"Eighteen miles wide!" Ethan breathes. We had barely gotten him out of the car because his game had charged just enough to turn on.

"I knew it would be big, but this puts big to shame," Sadie says as Mom and Dad walk by. I catch a sound with a metallic ping to it. The sun glints off something on the ground between Ethan and me. Ethan picks it up.

"Number 22..." He reads the block letters and number stamped on a small metal disk.

"Is it our campsite number?" Sadie asks.

Dad whistles a happy tune.

"Yep!" she says.

"What's that table over there?" Ethan points to the right. We inch in that direction through the crowds.

-3-

"The Society of Egyptian Preser...Preservation."
Sadie reads the sign. "What does that mean?"

Now we're trapped in the flow of people moving
toward the table, so we shuffle past, looking at pictures of a cave entrance and hieroglyphic writing. A
man is selling shirts that say, *Grand Canyon—Egyptian mummies, caves; I saw it all!* I pick up a sheet of
paper the man is handing out and begin to read a
reprint from a 1909 newspaper:

ARIZONA GAZETTE

Friday, March 12, 1909

G. E. Kincaid was the second man ever to

navigate the Colorado River through the Grand Canyon.

"Well, who was the first?" Sadie says, reading over my shoulder.

"I don't know! It doesn't say, but listen to this: Kincaid claims to have found a cave that contained mummies, Egyptian artifacts of gold, and many hieroglyphics."

"No kidding?" Ethan comments. "What is a mummy's favorite kind of music?" Ethan wiggles his eyebrows while we think about the answer.

"Um, silence?" Sadie finally says shrugging.

"No, *wrap* music, ha!"

I fold the sheet of paper and slip it into my back pocket. The man at the table tells someone that the T-shirts are only $22.99. The amazing part is that a bunch of people are buying them!

"Well, we saw Mather Point and got the campsite number. I guess it's about time to head to Desert View," I say.

"Yes! I am going to conquer level nine!" Ethan rubs his slim stomach. "But..." he sniffs the air. "What is that delicious odor? *Mmm*. I smell subs. Aunt Ruth, it's been like two hours since we ate. What do you say to a sub? Nice soft bread, crispy lettuce," he kisses his fingers like a French chef. "And hot sauce!"

Mom smiles, shaking her head. "When you put it that way, I say yes—except for the hot sauce."

"Oh, yeah! Yum-yum in my tum-tum."

By the time we get into the truck with the subs, my mouth is watering.

Ethan takes a bite, throws back his head, and groans. "What did I tell you? It's heavenly!"

I inhale mine at nearly the same rate as Ethan, but Sadie only gets half of hers eaten. I pull out the park map. It looks like nearly 30 miles to drive to Desert View, and Ethan is deep in his game after he wipes his mouth. I lean over to Sadie.

"Hey, are you gonna eat the rest of that sub?"

She looks at me flatly. "Yes. Just not right now."

"Bummer," I say, then Sadie takes one more bite.

"Ouch!" She holds her lip. "Something hard is in my sandwich!" I lean over and look as she opens the top roll of her sandwich.

"It's a key!" I shout.

"What's it doing in my sub?"

"Hiding!" Ethan snorts.

I pull it out and wipe it off, finding I can't move fast enough to get it into the little box. It slides into the keyhole perfectly.

"No way!" Sadie breathes. I turn the key, and the inside of the box snaps open. "What's in it?"

"It's…" I peer inside. "…a postcard?" I need a few tries to remove the slick, shiny thick paper. The postcard is of Wyoming, and it's been cut into a heart shape.

"Mom, Dad, what on earth is going on?" Sadie asks.

Mom just shrugs but then adds, "I would keep it safe if I were you."

That's all we can get out of them on the subject.

So, I sift through the brochures Sadie had grabbed at the Visitor Center.

"Wow, we could probably spend three full days just seeing everything in Grand Canyon Village."

"Look at this! Phantom Ranch is the only official place to sleep in the bottom of the canyon, and the mule ride stops there! I wonder if we'll get to sleep at Phantom Ranch," Sadie says.

Excitement tingles down to my toes. *What are Mom and Dad up to? And what is the pot of gold?* I can't wait to find out.

"Do you think there actually were Egyptians living in the Grand Canyon? I wonder if we'll find any artifacts," Sadie says.

"I don't know, but are you gonna eat the rest of that sub?"

She moves it off her lap and to her other side—out of my reach. Then she points and exclaims, "Desert View Campground!"

Sadie and I strain to see everything out of the window at once. I look over to find Ethan still glued to his game, missing everything. Huge, sharp-edged boulders are strewn everywhere amid short, scraggly Ponderosa pines.

"Nearly everything is rocks and sand," Mom comments.

One side of my mouth pulls back, remembering how the glitter in my sleeping bag at Rocky Mountains survival week had felt so sandy. Sadie and the girls in her cabin had pulled a prank involving glitter on all the boys in my cabin. Their practical joke is funny to me now—especially since I have a new sleeping bag from the deal. But I must admit, it wasn't funny then. A mischievous grin takes the corner of my mouth as I recall that week.

I elbow Sadie, "Hey, Sadie, are you gonna finish that sub?" She reacts exactly like I knew she would.

"Oh, Isaiah!" She makes an angry face, but I see a twinkle in her eye.

"Where are we going now?" Dad asks as he drives past the half-moon-shaped tent site then a rectangular RV site.

"22," Sadie and I say together, and I elbow Ethan in the ribs.

"What, oh, site 22 it is," he adds, then grimaces, "Nooooo!" He mashes the buttons on his game. "How could I lose after all that?" He slams his game down onto his lap and then sniffs the air. He looks at Sadie. "Oh, Sadie, are you going to eat that sub?" he asks.

"Eeeehh!" she yells, then stuffs a huge bite into her mouth. Clearly, she thinks she's going to get away from the question by eating the sub. I smile. *Not by a long shot!*

We pull into site 22, and I rush for my tent sealed tight in its bag in the back of the truck. Setting it up is one of my favorite tasks. When I have it just so, I finally let myself pull out my new hydration pack. I finger the double-insulated Camelbak water reservoir that holds 10 cups. I slide my arms into the straps and pull the hose up to my mouth. It's so fun to bite the end and sip cool water from it. It'll be perfect for the Grand Canyon's searing heat, plus it fits over the top of my trusty bear-slashed pack with four Junior Ranger badges on it.

"Isaiah," Sadie giggles, pointing at Ethan.

He's perched on a big red-and-tan streaked boulder, scowling at his game with his long legs folded up Indian-style. A blue jay is screaming at him, scolding him from a branch not far away. When he doesn't move, it dives at him, pulling up at the last second.

Ethan swats at it without looking up, completely absorbed in his game. The bird rockets toward him again, grabbing his hair this time.

"Ouch!" Ethan shouts, holding his head where a spike of hair is pointing skyward. He looks around but doesn't see anything and goes back to his game.

Sadie and I take a seat to watch the show. The bird is joined by another with less vibrantly colored feathers. They chatter at each other on a branch for a while and then dive for our unsuspecting cousin. The female grabs more hair with her claws and flaps wildly at Ethan's forehead. He drops the video game, screaming at the top of his lungs. He's slapping and flailing, but the bird is faster, and she is as angry as a hornet.

I'm laughing so hard I can't move. Mom rushes over. "Hey, you crazy bird, go away!"

The female jay flies up to a branch, but she doesn't stop scolding. Mom leans over Ethan, finds him whole, and heads back to finish setting up her camp kitchen.

As Sadie leans against me, tears of laughter roll down her face. But we soon discover the show isn't over yet.

As Ethan searches for his game, both birds dive again. This time he's ready for them, karate chopping like wild.

"*Wwwhhhaaaa! Ha!* I won't leave without my game!" he shouts.

The birds fly skyward, Ethan snatches his game and starts to run. The female tucks her wings, gaining speed. At the last second, right over his head, she swoops up, opens her rear hatch, and lands a bird-sized bomb on Ethan's back. *Splat.*

"*Eeehhhhaa!* I'm hit! I'm hit!" he screams, ripping off his shirt as he runs to shelter.

I can barely breathe, but Sadie squeaks out, "Run faster! She's coming again!"

Ethan launches for the unzipped tent door. *Splat.* The jay misses this time but not by much.

"That was better than a movie!" Sadie declares.

Later, after Ethan has advanced two more levels from the safety of the tent, Sadie freezes.

-4-

"A fox!" she whispers. I follow her pointer finger to see…*nothing*.

"Where?"

"Hold on, you'll see him when he moves. I think he's going to steal that man's bag of chips."

I shift quietly and then spot a small gray fox with one white front paw dart forward, snatch an open snack bag, and take off. His dark-tipped, bushy tail hangs down as he runs.

"Wow! He's fast! I was expecting a red fox; that's why I didn't see him," I say.

The fox stops, marks his territory with a pleased expression on his narrow face, then trots away.

"We'll have to be extra careful with our food. Did you know gray foxes have semi-retractable claws? They stay so sharp that they can climb trees. They have rotating wrists that turn, which also helps them climb."

"I didn't know that. Hey, you gonna eat the rest of that sub?"

Sadie shakes her fist at me, which makes me grin. She pulls out a sheet of notebook paper and starts writing while I stoke the fire and look over the brochure for the mule ride.

Movement one site over from ours catches my attention. The lonely tent unzips, and a boy near my age steps out. He frowns, then kicks a pebble, heading to the restroom that's near the end of our loop.

Ethan unzips our tent an inch or so, his bright blue eyes peer out, searching. "Are they gone?"

"Gone?" Sadie scrunches up her nose. "The blue jays have a nest in that tree right there, so they haven't gone far. But I think they've stopped hunting for you."

"Whew…"

"Mom took your shirt to the restroom and scrubbed it. I don't know that it helped much," I add.

"Thanks, Aunt Ruth!" Ethan calls. "It's a good thing she did. I only brought two shirts altogether."

"Figured." I shake my head. *That's Ethan—saving his packing space for his snacks.* "What did you bring this time?"

"Sunflower seeds."

I stare at him blankly. "Excuse me? You brought something healthy?"

"Aww, man, they are so salty!" He digs out a handful and stuffs them into his mouth, black and white shells and all. He looks remarkably squirrel-like as he works one between his front teeth, then spits out the tiny shells. "Want shome?" he slurs.

"Sure." I must admit it's fun to spit out the hulls.

"Hey," Ethan spits a shell after every word. "Who…whew…is that?" He points to our neighbor, who is returning from the restroom.

"Let's go find out." Sadie sets down her notebook, and we head toward the boy. Ethan pulls an atomic fireball candy from his pocket and pops it into his mouth.

So much for healthy.

The boy tries to veer off when he sees us coming, but a set of boulders prevents him. I introduce the three of us, but the boy still looks like a cornered animal.

"I'm Nate," he finally says without looking up. He kicks another pebble then makes a beeline for his tent.

"Nice fellow," Ethan says in a dry voice, then he fans his mouth from the hot candy.

"Where are his parents?" Sadie questions, looking around. "I haven't seen anyone but him all evening."

"That's odd, isn't it?"

-5-

My mule's name is Daisy. She looks nothing like a flower, but she is a LOT bigger than I figured she would be. Her huge ears swing toward me.

"Um. Hello," I say when she reaches for me with her wide gray nose. She stomps her front hoof, and dust rises from the ground.

"Easy there, Daisy." My nervousness shows in my quivering voice.

"Sable!" Ethan cries happily, striding right up to his mule and hugging her long face. Sable snorts when a fly lands on her nostril, and gunk rockets straight onto Ethan's chest.

"Okay, it's clear you aren't as excited about our

ride as I am." He plucks his long-sleeved shirt from his skin, hunching forward.

"Wrangler Higgins, you could have warned me about the possibility of this happening!" he says to the tough-looking man who will lead us into the canyon.

He's tall with skin like dry leather. He tips Ethan's hat back. "Why? You figured it out on your own just fine." Then he raises his voice. "Riders, mount up."

I move to Daisy's broad side and wonder which foot goes in the stirrup. *"Grrr."*

Pulling myself into the saddle is more awkward than hard. I look over to see Sadie already settled, happily petting her mule's neck.

Wrangler Higgins whistles, and the mules start forward on their own.

"Whoa!" I grab the saddle horn, then scramble to pick up the reins as we head toward the South Kaibab Trail.

"Something tells me these mules have done this

before," Ethan says. His mule cuts mine off, and the animals form a single file line.

It takes me a while to loosen my death grip on the saddle horn and enjoy the ride. Ahead of Ethan, a very loud lady is wearing a Grand Canyon, Egyptian mummies shirt.

"They carved out the caves with hand tools; Kincaid found one room deep inside filled with mummies and golden artifacts," she was saying.

I twist in my saddle to find Sadie behind me. "I wonder if we could find it."

"Kincaid's cave?" she asks, still stroking her mule's neck.

"Of course, we found gold in Zion, remember? Why not hunt down this legend too?"

She snorts. "Well, for one thing, the Grand Canyon is huge. Plus, the heat can be deadly. Then, oh, yeah, there's the Colorado River raging at the bottom that would we have to cross."

"You sure have a way with words," I mutter, sitting straight again just in time to catch sight of the rim. My mouth hangs open at the sight. Buttes and jagged peaks reach skyward from the depths of the canyon. The rocks are cleanly striped with red, tan, and cream. I'm not sure just how, but the Grand Canyon is like a universe all its own, replete with a different set of rules.

Heat waves make the air shimmer, but Ethan's mule has stumbled! No, the beginning of the trail down is that steep and makes it look as if the mule is falling.

"Whoa, Nelly! Or Sable, whatever your name is!" Ethan says as he leans back in his saddle, but now Daisy is shifting downward too, and I cling, white-knuckled, to the saddle horn again.

"Maybe we should think this trip over, Daisy!" I say, but she flat out ignores me. And now we have reached the point of no turning back from the Grand Canyon universe with its sharp drop-off, searing heat, and incredible beauty.

The trail we're on looks to be only six inches wide, and I force myself not to look down. Daisy's hoof strikes a pebble, and I count as it flings off the trail so I can gauge how deep the canyon is here. *Ping...ping...*then nothing... I lean toward the safety of the dusty rock face to the left. The canyon is so far down, I couldn't hear the pebble hitting!

"Okay. People do this all the time. We'll be fine. Right, Daisy?" My voice squeaks out her name.

"Uncle Greg!" Ethan shouts over his shoulder, "Where is my seat belt?"

Wrangler Higgins twists easily in his saddle at the front of the line. "Pipe down, young man. Trust me, nobody wants an excited mule on this set of switchbacks."

"*This set?* How many sets are there?" Ethan asks.

The wrangler simply grins with half his mouth and turns back around.

"What I really want to know is, how long will it be until I can play my video game?"

Wrangler Higgins twists back toward us, pinning Ethan with a steely look. "Best use for that nonsense, young man, is to throw it over the rim and count how long you can still see it or hear it hit the bottom."

Ethan turns toward me with an insulted expression. The trail soon consumes our every thought because it switches back on itself so sharply that each mule's head and neck swing way out over a mile of nothing below as they cross their front legs to navigate the turn.

"Think about it real hard, Daisy. That's right, don't trip now." I'm not sure if my advice helps her, but my heart is in my throat until she makes the turn, and we're headed down the next descent.

After five more switchbacks, it occurs to me that Daisy is pretty good at traversing this trail, so instead of hyperventilating every time she turns, I get the most incredible glimpses of the canyon possible with a mule's pointed ears to frame the picture forever burned into my mind.

We break for lunch at a place named Indian Garden. The place seems poorly named to me as there is little-to-no vegetation. By now my feet are numb, and I sure wish my seat in the saddle was too. "Ow."

"*Ehhh.*" Sadie grimaces as she hobbles forward. "Remember the last time we sounded like this at Rocky Mountain National Park?"

I nod. The promise I had made to her back then hasn't weakened. *We're family, and that's worth protecting.*

"Ouch!" I groan, as Ethan bumps me hard from behind.

"Oh, sorry, I didn't see you there," he says without pulling his nose from his screen.

"Maybe Wrangler Higgins was right. You should just throw that game away," I say, rubbing my shoulder.

He cradles it against his chest. "No way! I'm about to become a gold falcon!"

He's still playing it as we open our sack lunches, hiding from the searing heat in what little shade the cliffs provide.

A fat housefly buzzes around my head. I swipe

at it, so it flies to Ethan, bouncing repeatedly off his forehead. He blows air up at it, but he won't take his hands from the game control. His insulated water bottle sits open next to him. *Bzzzz.* The fly returns and hits his forehead so hard, it bounces off without a sound, landing with a plop right in Ethan's water.

"Yes, I made it! Look, it's so beautiful!" He stomps his foot happily on the rock and then goes back to playing.

"Should we tell him?" Sadie leans close, whispering.

I frown, studying him. "Naw, he should have noticed it himself."

"You're right," she agrees.

I crunch a handful of nuts and listen to the same woman who'd been talking earlier about the Egyptians. "They also found hieroglyphic writing near Lake Powell. You'd have to be crazy not to believe Egyptians lived here!"

A hiker is passing our mules, squeezing close

to us. I notice his shoes have some tough-looking tread, and his muscles are popping out everywhere. A bunch of carabiners and ropes neatly hang on his bright-green pack. He pulls out a water bottle and squirts his face. The woman keeps talking just like she's done the entire ride.

Sounding annoyed, the man butts in, saying, "You know, all that Egyptian stuff is a hoax."

-6-

"I don't see how you could possibly say such a thing," the lady's voice rises even louder.

"Have you seen any evidence of it yourself?" the hiker demands.

"I've seen all the pictures—incredible pictures!"

"Exactly," the man responds dryly. "Let me guess, the guy with the pictures was selling souvenirs, right?"

"No!" The woman's face is red—but not from the growing heat in the canyon.

"Well, where did you get that shirt from then?"

The woman clamps her mouth shut, glaring at the hiker.

He shrugs. "I'm telling you, it's a hoax. I've got proof."

"And why should people believe your so-called proof?" the woman snarls.

The hiker shakes his head and continues walking where he was originally headed.

"Dad, what is a hoax?" Sadie asks.

"It's a made-up story," he replies.

"But it's more than that; it's a story specifically designed to make people believe it. Usually, the person spinning the tale profits in some way from it," Mom adds.

"Do you think the Egyptian story is one of those hoaxes?" Sadie puts a potato chip in her mouth.

Dad shrugs. "I'm not sure. I've heard a lot about it, and the man with the booth was certainly very convincing. But the hiker is right; a picture isn't hard evidence."

Wrangler Higgins calls out, "Riders, mount up!"

We gather our garbage and stretch our sore muscles. Ethan carefully tucks his game into his pack. My eyes swerve to Sadie's as he takes a gulp of his water. Her grin turns into an all-out laugh as his eyes bug out. Water rushes out of his nose as he coughs, sputtering and gripping his throat with both hands.

"Ack!" He draws a ragged breath. "An insect! Ugh! I swallowed an insect!" He shudders, jigging to one side, and clutching his stomach. "I can feel it crawling in there!"

"Ethan," Dad says calmly, making me wonder if he had seen the fly fall in too. "Your stomach acid would kill it in seconds. Besides, it was most likely already dead."

Sadie bites her lip hard to keep from laughing as we head to our mules. Ethan is still hacking and spitting. "It tastes awful."

I mount the mule much easier this time and don't clutch the horn when Daisy starts forward. *I might be getting the hang of this mule riding.*

Up ahead, Ethan has started steadily hacking a loud, dry cough.

Wrangler Higgins scowls at him from his position ahead. "You might just be the loudest rider I've ever had in my string."

"Thank you, sir," Ethan says between coughs.

"Might start an avalanche…" Wrangler Higgins shakes his head.

An hour and a half later, we are still avalanche-free, and right ahead is a long suspension bridge over the brilliant blue of the Colorado River. I look up to see the canyon walls climbing high for a full mile. *A mile deep!*

The hooves of the first mule echo loudly on the bridge, and thankfully, the air over the river is just a hint cooler.

"That's Bright Angel Canyon straight ahead. Congratulations, you are at the bottom of the grandest place on earth!" Wrangler Higgins announces. "Y'all are welcome to dip your toes in the cool waters of Bright Angel Creek after we arrive at Phantom Ranch as well."

My first glimpse of Phantom Ranch makes my

skin tingle. It is a lush oasis with short, scrubby trees and wooden cabins hidden all around.

"Thank God we're here," Mom says, rubbing her legs before dismounting.

Ethan swings his leg over the mule's back, fails to catch himself, and lands flat on his back with his legs frozen upward—as if he is still in the saddle!

Wrangler Higgins walks over in his worn cowboy boots, kicking up dust. He puts his hands on his hips and says, "I suppose five and a half hours of hard riding will do that to a greenhorn like you."

Ethan gives a pitiful cough in reply. Not falling beside him takes all my determination. My ankles feel like they've been caught in vices.

"When's dinner?" Ethan asks as Dad and I haul him to his feet.

"They'll serve it soon at the Phantom Ranch Canteen. I believe steak is on the menu," Dad says.

"Order me a double. I'm so hungry I believe I could eat a mule."

Sable nods her giant head and lets out a half

whinny, half a donkey bray that makes us all cover our ears.

"Sorry, did I say that? I...I meant a cow, right? Steak comes from cows."

When we finally get settled in our cabin, we head to the canteen. I think I might faint when they bring out the food because it smells so good. The server slides a plate in front of me, but I see an odd-looking piece of paper stuck to the bottom.

"Ma'am, you forgot your list!" I say, but she's already heading back to the kitchen. I look around to see that no one else's plates have anything stuck to them. I slip out the paper and read the line written in a bold print: **Miss Mabel's Pie Is Missing**.

"What's that?" Sadie asks.

"*Ywlb.*"

I think Ethan meant to say *yeah*, but his mouth is full of steak.

"I don't know. It was left under my plate."

"Ish pie on the menub?" Ethan stuffs another bite in his mouth.

"I don't think so," Mom says, taking a bite and rolling her eyes.

I do the same. "Oh, it's so good."

"But why would she leave that note with just you?" Sadie presses.

"Blueberry..." Ethan swallows. "Or apple. No pumpkin pie. Yum!"

Sadie lifts her plate, and finding nothing, she elbows me. "Read the rest of it."

I clear my throat and begin to read. "Miss Mabel has always lived at Phantom Ranch. Yesterday, she spent hours preparing and baking the perfect pie..."

"Yum! It was peach! I know it," Ethan interrupts.

I stare hard at Ethan for a second then begin reading again.

"Her famous *blackberry* pies are worth more than gold down here in the bottom of the canyon. Around noon, she set the pie on the rock ledge to cool. She decided to go dip her toes in the creek to cool off after all that hard work. When she was walking back, she spotted a big bushy shadow near the ledge. She ran the rest of the way to check on her pie, but her worst fear was confirmed. *The pie was gone.*

"Three suspects immediately came to her mind. Big Bob Canteen, a huge man with a head full of wild red hair, loved her pies and had even asked for her hand in marriage last year. Miss Mabel had declined. She knew all he really wanted was to have pie whenever he liked.

"Another suspect was Trixie Rockford, who sure is pretty with all that curly blonde hair. Two years ago, Miss Mabel's blackberry pie had beaten Trixie's blueberry buckle in a contest, and things have been tense between them since. In fact, Miss Mabel now keeps her recipes in a locked box, and the key to the box is hidden under her pillow.

"The third suspect is Angel Willard, Miss Mabel's second cousin once removed. Last year, Angel had done Miss Mabel's laundry all spring for a payment of one pie. But Miss Mabel's pies were in great demand, and she needed her pie money to pay bills. Additionally, the blackberry crop hadn't been abundant that year. Miss Mabel had given away the last pie, and Angel had not received her promised payment. Plus, Miss Mabel couldn't stand Angel's bringing her pet raccoon with her! Not only had there been raccoon fur on her clean laundry, but Miss Mabel simply couldn't handle that creature's sitting on Angel's shoulder all the time—even during meals. What if Angel fed half of her pie to that varmint? Even though Miss Mabel knew the way she had treated Angel was wrong, she had many more favors to pay off, and she'd left Angel up a creek without a paddle.

"Who stole the pies?"

-7-

Sadie pins Mom and Dad with one of her looks. "Listen, we need to know just one thing. Should we give this note back to the server?"

"Oh, I wouldn't worry about it. I feel sure she doesn't want it back," Mom says.

Sadie quickly snatches the paper out of my hand and whispers, "I just know this has to be the next clue for us to solve."

"The only thing is…I don't have a clue how to solve it," I mutter.

"Clearly the *bushy shadow* is important." Sadie is absorbed with solving the riddle now.

Still, by the time we finish our dinner, we have

nothing new to go on—even though Ethan has asked our server if she knows a Miss Mabel.

"Clearly, this puzzle is meant to be solved here at Phantom Ranch. It's already evening, and we ride out early in the morning," I say, feeling the stress of solving the riddle quickly.

"Thanks for reminding me of the added pressure," Sadie says.

"Oh, no, dead battery!" Ethan whines, tucking his game back into his pack. "Wait, Big Bob Canteen? That's where we ate—at the canteen. Maybe we should go back and look for the pie there. I can't wait to eat it!"

"Well, that idea is better than nothing."

We head back to the Phantom Ranch Canteen with Mom and Dad lagging behind, holding hands and whispering.

"Still not a stitch of help from those two," Ethan huffs.

"Heard that!" Dad says happily.

We wander all around the restaurant without

success. Finally, we end up in the small gift shop. They don't have much to offer—just some snacks, water, bug repellent, and a nearly empty rack of postcards behind the counter.

"Duplex cookies!" Ethan exclaims. "Come to Papa!"

He takes the package to the counter, digging money from his pocket. "Ma'am," he says to the attendant, "you wouldn't happen to know a Miss Mabel, would you?"

The lady's eyes twinkle as she smiles sweetly and says, "I've never met her myself, but I hear she makes the best *blackberry* pies."

The three of us look at each other, and I nudge Ethan to keep going.

"Soooo, how about Big Bob Canteen, do ya happen to know him?"

"Sure, but I think we'll call him Bald Bob Canteen from now on. Ya see, he got a haircut yesterday morning."

"Bald Bob is out," Ethan whispers.

"And that haircut sure went wrong," the lady continues. "Anyway, he got a haircut because he was getting married yesterday at noon."

"Noon..." Ethan whispers again. "He was busy at the exact time of the crime, plus he's bald. Bob is double out."

"But you'll never guess who he got hitched to! Trixie Rockford! That woman can bake a mean dessert herself. I think they'll be happy together."

"Trixie's out."

"What did they have for dessert at the wedding?" Sadie asks.

"It was the best chocolate cake I ever ate, but you know the strange thing is that Angel wasn't even there—even though she and Trixie are good friends," the lady says.

"Shoot!" Sadie snaps her fingers.

"It was still good thinking," I whisper to cheer her up.

"Say, could I interest you in a postcard to go with these cookies?"

Ethan frowns at the nearly bare rack. "Looks like you've only got one."

"Well, you know, every single item here at Phantom Ranch must come in by mule. So, you can't blame us for not having much. Maybe you should just look."

She pulls down the card. Turns out three postcards were neatly stacked together. Two are pictures of the Grand Canyon.

"Maine?" Ethan asks, "why would you have a star-shaped postcard from Maine at the Grand Canyon?"

The woman smiles wide. "It does seem unusual, doesn't it?"

I pick up the star-shaped card. I notice that part of the lettering has been cut off to create the shape of a star. "It definitely wasn't printed this way," I mutter.

"It's custom for sure," the lady says.

"We'll take it," the three of us say in unison.

"The postcard is on the house." Then she lowers

her voice. "Case you didn't know, that means *free*. But the cookies are $2.99."

Ethan pays her, opens a pack, and stuffs all four cookies in his mouth at once.

"Y'all come back now. Sorry you missed the wedding."

We wave, and I catch Mom giving the lady a quick thumbs-up.

"I saw that!" I say flatly.

Mom clasps her hands behind her back and whistles a tune is if she hadn't heard me.

As soon as we're out of the restaurant, Sadie turns to Mom and Dad. "It was Angel!" she declares triumphantly.

"*Hmmmm...*" Dad shrugs, heading toward our cabin.

"Wait! Does that mean we're wrong?" I ask, but they won't respond.

"What are we supposed to do now?" Sadie's arms flop at her sides.

"Hold the phone," Ethan says.

"I don't have a phone," Sadie grumps.

"No, I mean, I have an idea. Bright Angel Creek. Plus, she has a raccoon, right? Raccoons like to wash their food before eating it, so I think we should check it out."

"Actually, that's a common misconception. Raccoons don't wash their food, but so much of what they eat comes from creeks, it often looks like they are washing it."

"Thanks for bursting my bubble, Sadie," Ethan says.

"You're welcome," she adds sweetly.

"Well, it's the only idea we have. Clearly just the name Angel wasn't what they were looking for. Let's go."

We hike down the small foot trail toward a shallow creek that waters the area. Mom has her bare feet in the cool water within seconds.

"Oh, it's wonderful!"

Soon we're all wading and splashing, having a blast.

"Shh…" We all freeze at Sadie's warning. "It's the fox! Remember the chip thief?"

I whisper, "It sure is! Look! He's got that white front paw."

She points into the underbrush, and after a minute, I spot a second fox. This one has no white markings at all. They play like puppies until Ethan sneezes. They take off like lightning had struck.

"Ethan…" Sadie groans.

"Sorry," he says, wiping his nose.

"Look!" Sadie cries, rushing to the far shore.

"It's a pie tin!" Ethan beats Sadie to it. "An *empty* pie tin." Only smears of purple berry remain on the bottom of the pan.

Ethan licks the tin, then his face screws up. "Gross!" He sniffs. "Aunt Ruth, is this purple paint? I wanted pie!" Ethan cries.

Mom covers her smile with her hand.

Ethan flips the pan over. "Aha! Here's the next clue."

-8-

"Let me see it," Sadie says.

"I'm the one who licked the purple paint, remember? Plus, I swallowed a bug today, so I think I deserve the honor of reading it aloud."

"The bug was your fault. So is the paint."

"How could you say such a thing?" Ethan's expression is horrified. "It's not like I threw that bug in my drink. Nor did I ask for his company...at all."

Sadie rolls her eyes. "You were so absorbed in your game that you failed to pay attention to your surroundings, which, if you'll remember from survival week, is incredibly important, King Shamrock."

Ethan presses his lips together, squinting at the name he had earned at Rocky Mountain National Park. "That was a low blow, Sadie Rawlings. *Low*."

"No, it wasn't. Do you realize how much of this trip you're missing because of your silly game?"

"*Silly?*" Ethan's voice squeaks out the word.

"Clue?" I step between them before things get any hotter.

Ethan lofts the pie tin and clears his throat.

A pledge ahead, a trail behind, a paper in between. The age of this canyon is the opposite of you. The rocks tell their own story.' Oh, there is a name for the study of rocks…hmm. If only we had a museum, we could probably remember it. Ya, we could. What rhymes with Ya? What about Va? Anyway, you did great figuring out who stole Miss Mable's pai. One last thing: you should probably ask us for something.

Love M & D, or for you Ethan, A & U."

"Va?" These clues keep getting weirder." I shake my head.

"Take it easy; you've got Ethan here. ETHAN, the clue solver."

"It's getting dark, ETHAN. Let's head to our cabin and study this clue there," Sadie says.

Our cabin is cozy and sparse, and that bed sure is calling my name after our long ride. Ethan frowns at his game.

"No, baby. You had plenty of battery at lunch." He pounds his thigh with his fist. "I must have forgotten to power it off. What good is 5 percent?"

"Anyway," Sadie is studying the bottom of the pie tin. "We need to work on this clue."

I ease onto the bed, but I'm so sore from riding that I stand back up and head over to her. "A pledge ahead, a trail behind, and a paper in between. That part is easy at least; it's the rest of it that's tough."

"Wait," Sadie says, her brown eyes like saucers. "What do you mean easy?"

I smile at her, drawing out the moment. "I mean

easy-peasy, clear as a bell. Say, Sadie, are you going to finish that sub?"

"*Argh!* Isaiah, so help me, that sub is long gone! What does this clue mean?" She's about to burst, so I give in.

"What is one thing we have done every single time we've gone to a national park?"

"Camped."

I roll my eyes. "Well, other than that."

"Hiked."

"Sadie, we've taken a pledge to protect wild places, remember?"

"Oh, we're Junior Rangers. *Right,* with paper in between, but what does the trail behind mean?"

I shrug. "Must be something to do with the Grand Canyon's Junior Ranger program."

"Look! The age of these rocks is the opposite of you. We are not old, we're...*juniors.*"

"Exactly," I say as if I'd already figured that part out. "Ethan, you had better hurry, or we'll have the whole puzzle solved without you."

He groans, twisting his upper body hard as his thumbs fly. "No. Not now! You fickle battery, how could you leave me right here?" He flops back on his bed, arms spread wide. "Fine. We need to work on the last half of the clue. *Ya Va? Va Ya?* We're missing something here."

"Plus, we can't forget they misspelled pie. What could *pai* mean?" Sadie chews her lip.

"Hang on, what is the study of rocks called?" I search my brain for the word, but it floats around, just out of reach.

"Rockology?" Sadie says.

Ethan smacks his forehead repeatedly. "Come on...it's something with a J... Ju... No. It's a G. Geology!" He sits up.

"That's it!" I say.

"Why would we need a museum to figure that out?" Sadie wonders.

"Maybe it's not that we need a museum. Maybe it is a museum. Is there a geology museum in the park?"

"I left my maps and brochures at our tents! Now we can't figure it out until tomorrow night when we get back."

"But what is the question we're supposed to ask?" I cross my arms as Mom comes back from the shower room.

"That feels better! Your turn, Greg. You kids will need to get cleaned up too."

"Mom, what is the question?"

She smiles as she hugs me. "I have the answer, honey—not the question."

As we come back from the showers, Ethan shocks Sadie and me. He spreads his arms wide. "Wait!" he yells. *I'm searching everywhere for a rattlesnake or a cougar.* "I've got it."

I put my hand over my heart. "Don't do that again."

"You can thank me later. It's paper. Paper in between. What paper do we need to take a pledge? We need our Junior Ranger booklets!"

"That's it!" Sadie shouts, rushing after Dad as he

steps into our cabin. "Dad." We all pile through the door.

"Can we please have our Junior Ranger booklets?" Ethan asks.

Mom and Dad grin. "That's the right question," Dad says as Mom pulls the three booklets out of her bag.

"Yes!" Sadie says, taking hers and batting her eyes. "What does *Ya Va* mean?"

Dad tries to frown but doesn't quite make it. "That is not the right question. All right, you've got five minutes to look through your books, then it's lights out. We've got a big day of riding to get back to the rim tomorrow. The ranger told us it would be good for you to study your pages down here at Phantom Ranch so you can gather your answers on the way out. These are Grand Canyon Explorer books. The only way to earn this badge is to have hiked or ridden a mule to the bottom of the canyon."

"Cool!" I say. Then I flip through the book, finding plenty of questions that I don't know the answers to. Sadie has her Junior Ranger booklet and her notebook out. Ethan plugs in his beloved racing game, and I sigh long and deep as I lie down.

"*YAVA VAYA AAVY YAAV.*" I'm asleep before Ethan can finish combining all the letters.

-9-

We stop at Indian Garden for lunch again, and I nearly pull an Ethan when I dismount Daisy.

"Those are muscles I didn't know I had," Ethan squeaks as he hobbles toward a boulder. Wrangler Higgins, with his bowlegged knees, walks past and slaps Ethan's shoulder affectionately. "Enjoy the break, Greenhorn. We've got two and a half hours more to the top."

"Is that supposed to be encouraging?"

"Depends on how you look at it, I suppose." Wrangler Higgins stomps off, and I think I understand why he walks the way he does. I plunk next to Sadie on a rock.

"I'm so hungry I could eat five of the sack lunch-es they gave us," I say.

She takes a bite of granola bar. "Just so you don't ask about my sub," she says dryly.

"Well…" I elbow her. "Are you going to eat it?"

"*Agrh!*" She makes an angry face that quickly melts into a grin.

Ethan makes a long wailing cry that makes everyone look at him. "Are you all right, Greenhorn?" Wrangler Higgins asks.

"No. My battery didn't charge last night. I've got to conquer level 22!"

Wrangler Higgins just shakes his head.

Ethan wanders over. "Isaiah, don't you have a flashlight you can charge by cranking a handle?"

"Yeah," I answer cautiously, wondering why he wants it.

"Can I please borrow it?"

"For what?" I hedge. "It's broad, hot, daylight."

"Come on, please?"

"Fine."

I dig it from my pack and hand it to him, leaving a sweaty handprint on it.

"Thanks." He heads back to his boulder, plugs his game charger into the USB port on the flashlight, and cranks the tiny handle.

"You should have said no." Sadie says, searching the distance with her small binoculars.

"Yep." I watch him crank like crazy, knowing how quick the motion tires out your hand. Sweat drips as he increases his pace.

"1 percent... Go, baby, go," he mutters.

Sadie pokes me in the shoulder.

"Ow."

"Shh. Our *friend* is back...just past the mules."

The gray fox with a white front foot slips closer, darting from boulder to boulder.

"I call him One Paw. Look! He smells our food."

One Paw is like a shadow as he sneaks under the belly of Dad's mule. Ethan cranks faster, his hand a blur of motion. "Teeennnn percent. Yes!" He's drenched with quick-drying sweat from the effort, but he's completely focused on his game as he shifts his lunch aside and settles in to play.

One Paw's tiny nose tests the air, and his incredibly bright gaze falls on Ethan all by himself on the boulder. One Paw completes two cautious circuits of Ethan's boulder. He seems to shrink a little. Sadie gasps, grabbing my arm as he leaps up right behind Ethan.

"Should we do something?" she whispers.

The fox is so small—only the size of a large house cat. He's not aggressive in any way as he lifts his white paw to step forward, then hesitates, waiting for the right moment to slip away with Ethan's lunch bag.

Ethan is hunched, shielding his screen from the searing light, oblivious to One Paw. Sadie and I look at each other.

"Naah!" we say together.

The fox takes the step, darting forward to snatch Ethan's white lunch bag. One Paw spins to run, but at the edge of the boulder, he looks back over his shoulder, lunch bag dangling. Ethan hasn't moved an inch. With a wily look in his eye, the fox slinks back to Ethan, lifts his hind leg, and marks Ethan's back forever as his own territory.

"Sadie, stop it," Ethan says, completely focused on his game.

We burst out laughing.

"Wh…What? It wasn't me."

At Sadie's belly laugh, Ethan turns.

"Hey!" Ethan is on his feet in a heartbeat. One Paw leaps off the boulder and disappears, the paper sack swinging wildly from his mouth.

"Crazy fox, where's my lunch? Hey!" Ethan circles, pulling his white shirt around his thin waist until he can see the yellow stain.

"Wait. Did he use me for a bathroom?"

I slap my leg, trying to get the words out past my laughter. "N…not only will yo…you officially be a Junior Ranger, bu…but you'll now belong to One Paw forever!"

Wrangler Higgins shakes his head. "Never seen

such a thing." Then, in a louder voice, he adds, "Listen up, riders! It's time to take on the rim. Temperature is at 102°, so take another drink and watch for signs of heatstroke like we covered in our initial safety meeting. The Grand Canyon rescue teams deploy an average of 265 times per year, and we sure don't want that to happen on this mule ride."

"But I'm still hungry." Ethan insists, holding his wet shirt away from his body.

"Not my fault you were too busy gawking at that screen to protect what was yours, and I'm referring to both your lunch and your dignity."

"Eh? I had little dignity to start with, but I wanted my lunch."

Wrangler Higgins frowns and pats Ethan's mule on her wide head. "Just a little longer, girl."

My tongue is sticking to the roof of my mouth when Daisy's front hoof hits the flat of the southern rim. "Good girl," I croak. *One thing's for sure, the trail up would've beaten me. Between the steep switchbacks and the heat, I probably would have been a rescue call myself.*

Dad hands out more water as we gather under the shade near the barn. "I'll run and turn on the truck to let it cool down," Dad says.

Ethan fans himself, sweat drying before it can cool him. "Sweet! Ice-cold air conditioning!"

Sliding into Dad's truck feels like heaven. "Ahh."

"You kids did an amazing job. That was a real adventure, and you didn't complain once," Mom says. Dad clears his throat, and Mom adds, "Okay, maybe one of you did complain a little."

"Wet on by a fox," Ethan mutters, "how could I *not* complain?"

"How about some cold drinks?" Dad asks.

"Yes!" we shout.

-10-

Back at site 22, the heat has built inside the tents to an unbearable level, so we flop in the shade of some stubby pine trees on the far side from the jay's nest.

Sadie is writing in her notebook.

"What's that?" I ask. Ethan had charged his game in the truck though Dad hadn't been thrilled to let him, so he's in the sweltering tent playing.

"I've been tracking all the animals I've seen on this trip and recording where they were."

We both look up at the sound of one rock pinging off another.

"Hello?" I call, hating to leave our circle of shade.

Nate's forehead and eyes appear over a boulder. Then he sinks back out of sight.

"Hey," Sadie calls, "why don't you come over?"

We listen for a response, but all I hear are the blue jays attacking an innocent camper walking past.

"Maybe he didn't hear me," she says.

Then Nate's voice reaches us. "Why?"

"Because we're better company than rocks, *I think*," Sadie says with a giggle.

Nate looks over the boulder again.

"What did you do today, Nate?" I ask to ease his nerves.

"Nothing," he says, kicking another rock. His face is red from the heat.

"You mean you literally stayed in your hot tent all day?" Sadie asks, blinking rapidly.

"That's all I ever get to do here."

"Ever?"

"Yeah, my dad usually gets back after dark."

"From where?" I ask, curiosity eating at me.

"Uh, work," he says, dropping his eyes.

"Hey, are you any good at figuring out riddles?" Sadie asks.

"I don't think so. I mean, I don't know."

"Well, come on and give it a shot. We need help. Our parents have set us on a treasure hunt of sorts, and this clue is tough."

We explain the clues and adventures we've had so far.

"Your parents actually did all that—just for fun?" Nate asks in awe.

"Sure," Sadie replies easily, as she spreads out her maps and brochures. But I can see the shock and longing mixing in Nate's face. I feel bad for him, being so lonely in this incredible place. I hand him the pie tin and watch as he studies it.

"They misspelled pie."

"Exactly. It's a clue."

"To what?"

"I wish we knew."

"Oh."

As we sift through the maps and the various

brochures we have collected, Ethan eventually joins us.

"Your battery must be dead," Sadie surmises.

"Nope, the heat is getting to me, and I'm lowering my high score. I better wait until after dinner when I'm at my best."

She rolls her eyes.

"Well," I say as I study the map, "we've heard that the canyon is like a mountain, but in reverse. After today, I believe it. Going way too far down and not being able to hike back out would be easy."

"But the mule did all the work!" Sadie says.

"Not all of it," Ethan says, rubbing his legs.

"I got it!" Nate cries happily.

"How many times have you been to the bottom?" I ask, wondering if he meant he gets the upside-down mountain thing as well.

"Never. That's not what I'm talking about. I figured out the clue!" The smile on his face is the first one I've ever seen. He turns the glossy brochure toward us. "Yavapai Geology Museum!"

"Yes! Great job, Nate! You figured that out in less than 60 seconds!" Sadie holds out her hand for a high five.

"It's perfect because we can turn in our Junior Ranger booklet there and take our pledge," I add.

I search for the museum on the map. "But we'll probably have to do it tomorrow. When does the museum close?"

Nate scans the brochure. "It closes at 6:00 p.m."

I check my watch. "It's 5:45 right now. We won't have time to even drive there."

"Hey," Ethan says, "you could come with us tomorrow, Nate."

"Really? You would want me to come?"

"It would be fun!" Sadie exclaims.

"Well, thanks, but I don't think my dad would let me go."

"Just sitting here all day must sort of...stink," Ethan says.

"Like your shirt?" Sadie teases.

"I changed it."

"So, you're on your last shirt?" I ask.

"Nope, this one is Uncle Greg's. The blue jay ruined the first one beyond recovery, and One Paw got the second."

I look at Nate to find he's returned to his normal sour look. *I wish I could fix it.*

"Anyway, you're the one who figured out the clue. Will you at least ask?" I say.

"I will, but I already know the answer. I should head back now."

"See you."

As the sun fades beyond the largest canyon in the world, Ethan says, "Something weird is going on with Nate. What parent would take his kid camping at a national park and leave him in the tent all week?"

"It's fishy for sure."

A shadow flits overhead as Ethan flinches. "It's the mama jay, run!"

I hear an angry cry as we scramble to gather everything.

"She's going to drop one!" Ethan shrieks. "Not on Uncle Greg's shirt!"

But the blue bomber tucks in her wings as Ethan sprints for the tent. Sadie and I break in the other direction, circling wide.

"The tent is still zippered!" Sadie points at Ethan as he fumbles for the tab. *Splat!*

"Noooo!"

Right in the hair. Gross!

-11-

"Why wouldn't Nate's dad let him come?" I ask, enjoying the truck's air conditioning the next morning.

"I don't know, Isaiah," Dad responds. "I'd have asked him myself except I've never seen the man."

I gasp. "Do you think Nate is actually here by himself?"

"No, the park wouldn't allow a minor to rent a site, but it seems strange, doesn't it?" Dad says as we pull into the Yavapai Geology Museum.

"Don't forget your booklets," Mom calls. "They didn't get wet in the rain last night, did they?"

"No, they're good," Sadie says.

"Did you know that was the first rain they've had in a solid month in the canyon?" Dad asks.

"Wow! That's a long time. I guess that's why so few plants grow here."

The museum is full of exhibits explaining the different layers of rock in the canyon, but the big topographical map really draws me. I run my finger over the miniature canyon rim, amazed at how deep it is even on the 3-D map. The thrill of my first sight of it returns when we line up at the huge windows perched right at the edge of the rim.

We stand there for a long time, simply absorbing the wonder. After we have checked out the exhibits, Mom says, "Let's walk down to Yavapai Point Amphitheater for a ranger-led program. Then you all can get your badges."

Sadie, Ethan, and I whisper as we take the short trail. "What could the pot of gold be?"

"What happens if we don't find it?"

"Do your mom and dad ever stop holding hands?" Ethan adds.

"I heard that," Dad says as we reach the amphitheater.

"Wow! Did you notice the rocks embedded in the railings>" I run my hands over the different types. Some are smooth, some are dark-red, and some are ridged.

"Vishnu schist. Interesting," Ethan notes as we take a seat.

A ranger named Kevin explains the different types of formations we can see straight ahead in the canyon. It's easy to spot the temple formations because they are wide at the base and squeeze up to a point at the top.

Ranger Kevin adds, "To the left, you can clearly see the butte that's tall and flat-topped. Often, you'll see smaller towers all around them as well."

Ranger Kevin finishes his presentation, and we hand him our books. "Great, three new Grand Canyon explorers." He looks carefully through our booklets. "Which one of you is Ethan?"

"That would be the handsome one," Ethan says.

Ranger Kevin looks back and forth between Ethan and me, clearly not wanting to insult either of us.

"It's me," Ethan adds.

"Can you look at this answer right here?" Ranger Kevin hands Ethan his book.

"Oh, right. That one."

I look over and find one question that says: what type of rock is shiny and breaks into very thin layers? Ethan had written *Chevy.*

"Well, you see, my favorite car is a Chevy, and it's the one I drive in my *Road Tron* game. But I meant to write schist, sir." Ethan's become a bit humbler now.

"That's better." Ranger Kevin signs our books and asks us to raise our right hands. As we repeat the pledge to protect preserve and study the canyon, a deep peace settles over me just like it always does when I earn a Ranger badge.

"You are officially Grand Canyon Explorer Rangers. Congratulations! We will have to get your badges at the museum. Come on, I'll walk along with you."

"Sir," I ask, "do you think there are any Egyptian artifacts in the canyon?"

"Well, I've spent a lot of time in the park, and that's an understatement. But in all that time, I've never seen any. Neither has any other ranger that I know of." He shrugs. "But there is something I do know."

"Well, what's that?" I respond.

"Every year the park receives packages of all sorts. Sometimes there's a rock from the canyon or a piece of driftwood someone had plucked from the river. But one thing about the packages is always the same—the reason why the people return what they had taken. Without fail, they tell us to please take back the artifact they deeply regret taking because nothing has gone right for them since that item has been in their possession. Some folks even claim the artifact has nearly killed them."

"That is really strange," Dad agrees.

"Yes, it is," Ranger Kevin pulls open the door of the museum for us.

The ranger behind the welcome desk hands us our badges.

"Wow!" I exclaim. "It's my coolest badge yet with a scorpion ready to strike!"

"They glow in the dark too," Ranger Kevin adds, then he waves goodbye.

Sadie flips her badge over. "Look! Taped to the back of my badge is a note!"

-12-

Congratulations on your fifth Junior Ranger badge! We are so pleased with all you've learned and accomplished. So is Fred! He has got a special treat for you—one of Ethan's favorites. Today I saw some clouds that sure looked like whipped cream, nice and cold. It made me hungry for my favorite food too! Hurry up and figure out this clue!

Love, Dad

"Looks like we'll be needing that." I point to a big wooden sign with glass covering a map. We step outside into the heat and huddle in the sign's shade. Ethan runs his finger along the canyon. "Fred. Fred. Who is that?" he mutters.

"I don't think we know anyone named Fred, so it must be someone in the park," Sadie adds.

"Or something. Did you notice he kept mentioning food," I ask.

To the right, a large group of people have gathered around the Society of Egyptian Preservation. We watch as a ranger waves his arms. "Mr. Sanders, you're not allowed to sell anything in the park. We've had this conversation before, and if you don't listen, we will be forced to ban you from the Grand Canyon."

Eventually the crowd thins, and Mr. Sanders loads his table and shirts into his old truck.

"Whipped cream…" Ethan interjects.

"Dad's favorite food is a burger and fries," I finish my thought.

"Whipped cream…" Ethan says again.

"This map doesn't list any restaurants. Let's go ask inside," Sadie says.

"A banana split. Three flavors of ice cream covered in whipped cream with three cherries on top!" Ethan sprints past us for the main museum door. "Excuse me, ma'am, but I find myself in need of a banana split. Do you know anywhere in the park we could get one?"

The ranger grins at Ethan's desperate tone. "The only place I know of is Fred Harvey Burger."

"Aha! That's it, Fred!"

"Yes," I say, giving Ethan a fist bump.

"Dad, take us to Fred Harvey Burger!" Sadie exclaims when they step through the doors.

"Yes, ma'am. That was fast, but I'm hungry, so let's hurry."

The double bacon burger is the best I've ever had. All of us are rolling our eyes and moaning about how good the food is.

"I think we were all ready for a big meal," Mom says, smiling at us when Dad heads to the restroom.

Ethan inhales his burger in massive bites. "Aunt

Ruth, please don't tell me you were kidding about the whipped cream…"

Mom smiles. "You all can order a dessert today! Sadie, they have an entire list of sugar-free ice cream for you."

"Yes!" Ethan shouts, completely oblivious when everyone in the restaurant looks at him.

A while later, I'm smiling down at a triple scoop of strawberry ice cream with sprinkles on top. And Sadie is slurping up a sugar-free chocolate masterpiece. Ethan fidgets, falling short of patience as he waits for his split.

"Oh, there it is. Look at that beauty! It must be a foot tall!"

The server sets it in front of him, and I spy one corner of a paper peeking out beneath the big silver ice cream tray.

"You got something extra there," I say.

"No, sir, there won't be any extra. If you wanted one, you should have ordered your own." He plunges his long spoon deep through the whipped cream into the banana and ice cream beneath. He stuffs the spoonful into his mouth, shuts his eyes, and falls limply into his chair. "Heavenly!" he whispers around a mouthful, nearly losing his Maraschino cherry.

"I meant underneath your bowl," I insist, eyeing the shiny paper as I lick my cone.

"You'll just have to keep wondering. I need to focus on the sundae before it melts," Ethan says.

"Ethan…" Sadie pegs him with a look, chocolate sauce dripping from her spoon.

"Fine!" He stuffs in another massive bite. "Let's see." He shifts his heavy tray and reveals another postcard!

-13-

"What does it say?" Sadie leans forward.

"Indiana; it's cut into an oval shape." Ethan holds it out for us to see.

I take it and study it before handing it to Sadie. She tucks it carefully into her notebook with the others.

"Three strangely shaped postcards, a pot of gold, and a treasure hunt. Best. Vacation. Ever!" she declares, then shovels in more sugar-free ice cream.

"I'm glad you are all enjoying it," Dad says as he sits back down. "Something's surely special about the Grand Canyon!"

"It's like this place belongs to a different world. I wonder if we'll get in some paddling on the Colorado River?" I ask.

"You'll just have to take a clue!" He grins as he puts his arm around Mom.

"But we are out of clues," I press.

"They have a way of popping up, though, don't they?" The twinkle in Mom's eye tells me there's no way I'm getting any more information from them. I lick up the last of my dessert and sit back. "I'm cool and full—two things that are easy to take for granted on a normal day."

"Camping has been really good for us," Mom says, wiping her mouth with her napkin. "I've enjoyed the changes in myself and you three as well. Who would have guessed that you would be certified survivalists?"

"Not me!" Sadie agrees.

"And to think, I really wanted to go to the Smithsonian last fall." Mom nods.

"I knew it," I mutter, remembering the incredible feeling of her telling us we were going to the Grand Tetons instead. "Thanks, Mom."

"It was this close..." She holds up her fingers with barely any space between them. "But look at what we would've missed! Each national park has its own amazing sights and experiences. And now I can start a fire in less than two minutes."

"I can almost sleep through a raging stampede," Dad says.

"I can make a rope from the forest!" Sadie grins.

"I can be tortured by a multitude of wild creatures." Ethan slumps in his chair, and we burst out laughing.

"Glad you all think it's funny," he mumbles.

"You have to admit, on this trip you could have avoided the first blue jay bomb, the bug you swallowed, and your new ownership by a fox named One Paw with only one simple action," Sadie says.

"And what would that be?"

"Putting away your video game."

He frowns, so I add, "You know, at the Rocky

Mountains, all the kids thought you were the best thing since *sliced* bread?"

"Yeah," he says happily, running a hand through his hair.

"Well, you plus video games are like the best thing since *stale* bread."

"Is that a compliment or an insult? Because my mom makes the best stuffing from stale bread."

"It was an insult, Ethan. The game is stealing who you are from you," I insist.

"What do you mean?"

"It's stealing your time in one of the most incredible places on earth, it's stealing your thoughts, and it's turning your brain into mush."

"Mush, huh? Who figured out the Miss Mabel mystery?"

"You. But it was also you who got marked by a fox because you are so oblivious to the real world."

"You do have a point there."

"So…you're going to stop playing, right?"

"Not a chance."

Sadie and I groan together.

"All right," Mom stretches. "I agree, Ethan. The game is stealing from you. But for now, let's head out for a short hike, then we can get in our tents early tonight. I bought sugar-free marshmallows."

"They have those now?" I ask.

"Yep, and I intend to roast some tonight."

We don't drive very far toward Desert View when Sadie shouts, "Dad, pull over! We've got to stop here!"

I look at where she's pointing and see a park ranger with a huge bird sitting on a perch next to him. The crowd gathered around him is asking questions.

"It's a California condor!" Sadie adds excitedly.

Dad slows down to read, "Shoshone Point Trail, 2.1 miles. I don't believe this trail is listed on the map, but it looks perfect, plus there's this...*um*... ugly bird to see."

"Daaad!" Sadie cries, "He is not ugly! He's...sort of cute."

"Nope, he's ugly, but somehow that makes me want to look at it more closely."

I study the huge black bird as Dad parks. His head and neck are bald, and the leathery skin is yellow. The strangest thing about him is that his beak looks so strange because the yellow skin covers half of it, making the bird look as if he's a frowning old man with no teeth!

"I have to agree with Dad; he's ugly," I state as we get out.

"Aww, come on; he's amazing!" Sadie has her hands on her hips.

"It's the perfect moment to shock her, so I say, "Hey, Sadie, are you gonna finish that sub?"

"*Argh!*" She throws her hands into the air.

"Nice one," Ethan whispers.

We listen to the ranger, who says, "The California condor is one of the rarest birds in the world. In fact, in 1987 there were no more condors in the wild. Through captive breeding programs, we now have six stable wild populations in the U.S."

The bird bobs his very ugly head, with spiky black feathers at the base of his neck. Then he shifts to one end of the perch, spreading his wings for balance.

"Whoa!" Everyone ducks.

The ranger chuckles at our reaction. "California condors have a wingspan of nearly ten feet. They can reach the weight of 26 pounds, making them the second heaviest bird in America. Who can tell me how long a condor can live?"

"12 years," someone says.

"25."

People continue to shout out their guesses.

"Think higher. These birds can live to be 60 years old. Not too bad for a bird that eats carrion. Thanks for coming to see Edgar today and remember to respect all things wild."

The crowd breaks up, and we start down the trail. It's flat, easy hiking and the view from the plateau is amazing. We're nearly back to the truck when Sadie gets a stone in her shoe.

Dad rubs his belly. "That was a good burger. You think we ought to walk this trail again?"

I study him for a moment and then answer, "Noooo. Why would we?"

He shrugs. "I just hate for you to miss anything, you know."

I squint at him. "What do you mean by that?"

Dad shrugs again, so I know he won't say anymore. I turn to Sadie, who's getting her shoe back on. "Ethan, come on. Listen up, we missed it."

"Missed what?" Sadie asks.

"The next clue."

"How do you know?" Ethan asks.

"Because Dad just told me without telling me."

"Ooohhh."

"He said we might want to take this hike again."

"I didn't see anything," Ethan declares.

"Obviously. We've got to keep our eyes open. This time it could be anything."

"I didn't even have my game on," Ethan insists.

"We've still got to find it," Sadie says.

We set out back the way we came. I spin to look at Dad, but he and Mom are whispering as they follow way behind.

"Hey, look! A tiny arrow made from rocks is pointing toward this little trail," Sadie says, turning toward a faint trail. We follow it a short way to a small rocky outcropping.

"There," Sadie whispers and points. We catch movement up ahead. "It's One Paw." Her voice barely covers the distance between us. The crafty fox is working his way up an incredibly steep section of the canyon.

Sadie holds Ethan back. "Easy now. It was your fault for being such an easy target."

He grumbles as the fox disappears behind some boulders ahead. We sink down, but only flashes of gray fur appear now and then; he's moving so fast. He stops just ahead of us, only his bushy tail showing. One Paw turns toward us, and he's got something in his mouth!

"Is that our clue?" My voice rasps the question,

and a familiar feeling that warns me about danger races through my chest…except *there's no danger here.*

"The petty little thief," Ethan whispers. One Paw hasn't spotted us yet.

"It is our clue," Sadie whispers.

"That's it!" Ethan growls, then he explodes from our cover, shouting, with his long arms high in the air. His sudden appearance and sheer volume shock the fox into a frozen crouch.

Ethan leaps a boulder, shouting like a pirate, *"Aarrrhhh!"*

-14-

The fox drops the clue and takes off running. By the time Ethan reaches the clue, the animal is long gone.

"Victory!" Ethan lofts the floppy piece of material high.

"What is it?" Sadie is like a jackrabbit as she rushes forward to look.

"It might be a scrap of backpack material or something." Ethan frowns at the light-green material with ragged and limp edges.

"Wait! Something is written on it."

Ethan frowns. "He…Help me."

We stare at each other for a minute.

"That's it? What kind of clue is that?" I gripe, feeling the pinch of such a hard quest.

When Ethan flips the fabric over, I notice his fingers now have a pale, white dust on them. "Yep, that's it. *Help me.*"

Sadie sighs. "All right, what else can we gather from the clue? It looks like it was written in… chalk. See, it's all over your fingers."

"Right, but right here at the bottom, there's a darker stain."

On a closer inspection, I see Ethan is right. There is a small blotch of dusky brown against the lighter material.

"So, possibly it's a map? And the blotch is the goal?" I say.

"But there are no directions or anything." Ethan is frustrated.

"Okay, let's take it easy. We've got three noggins here that are fantastic at figuring out stuff like this. Being upset will only slow us down. Remember what Jim said at survival week? A positive mental outlook is the most important element you can bring to any situation."

"This is hardly a survival situation," Ethan mutters quietly.

"Well, it's *clue survival*, anyway. Let's search the area. Maybe One Paw didn't get the whole thing."

We search in the direction One Paw came from, but we come up empty-handed.

"Nothing," I say with sweat trickling down my forehead into my eyes.

"Let's head back to site 22 and work on this there. Your dad let us know when we completely missed it, so surely, he'll do it again if he needs to." Sadie carefully rolls up the clue and puts it in her pack.

"The point is not to need it," I say as we trudge back to Mom and Dad.

"Ready to go?" he asks easily.

Sadie, Ethan, and I exchange frustrated glances. "Sure," I say.

By the time we get to Desert View, I've already

rearranged the letters in the "Help me" note in every conceivable way. Elma. He. Meep—which I suppose is not a word, but I'm getting desperate.

"I need a trip to the restroom," Ethan says.

"Yeah."

The three of us trudge to the restrooms, the clue weighing us down. We regroup and head back.

"Do you hear that?" Sadie says.

Faint voices reach us. We creep forward until we can hear them clearly.

"It's called a hoax, Nate," a sharp voice accuses.

"Yeah, he's a fake—just like you, Nate," another voice says. I hear the scuffling of feet and then a grunt.

"All right, that's enough," Ethan says, his mouth set in a firm line. He strides around the boulders and confronts the guys. "Hey, boys, take your problem somewhere else."

Ethan's height and sudden appearance give him an intimidating advantage, but I step out behind him just the same.

Three other boys my age sneer at us. "Yeah, he's not worth the effort." One of them kicks a rock our way, which Nate leaps away from.

When the boys are gone, I turn to find Nate with dirt smudged on his cheek, and his eyes red-rimmed.

"You all right?" I ask.

He shrugs. "They're from my school." He sighs heavily. "And they make my life miserable—even in the summer."

"Not with us around. Come on, Nate, we've got another clue," Sadie adds.

We settle around the campfire, sitting far from the heat but within its circle of light. Sadie pulls out the scrap of heavy fabric and hands it to Nate.

His face goes pale as he stares at it.

"Nate, are you all right?" I ask.

"Um…I gotta go." He hands me the clue and takes off for his lonely site. Dad watches him go.

"Well, he didn't stay long. Is everything good?"

"I think so." I say. I bend over to study the letters

again. None of the words I have formed from the letters make more sense.

"Hey, you know the letters are speckled, almost lighter colored—like rain has hit them," I say, drawing Ethan and Sadie nearer.

"You're right. And look, since we've been handling it, we're getting the chalk all over it. It's messy now."

"We better be more careful," Ethan says, pulling out his game.

"So much for your help," I say, but he doesn't even respond.

I hover my finger over the letter H. The writing is about the same width as my pointer finger.

"Looks like Dad used his finger to write this—not a brush or something else."

"Good point," Sadie says.

I struggle with the shrieking warning in my chest, reasoning it away. As Sadie and I get smack dab to the middle of nowhere, working on the clue.

-15-

Morning dawns soft and pink. I slip out of the tent and watch the world wake up. All night a heavy sense had pushed in on me as I thought about the clue. It's no use asking Dad for help. We've got to figure it out. Still, something's just not right, but I can't put my finger on it. *What are we missing?*

With barely a whisper of sound, Sadie is suddenly beside me.

"Did you sleep?" she asks.

"Not much."

"Me neither. I kept dreaming of someone crying, 'Help me.'" She shivers and hugs her knees.

"There's just got to be something we're missing," I say.

As soon as the sun is up, the heat builds. We flinch at a metallic ping in the silence.

"What on earth?" Sadie points at Ethan.

"I can't believe what I'm seeing! Is that a garbage can lid on his head?" I whisper.

"And another he's using for a shield? What's he got around his stomach?"

I laugh as I answer, "It's shiny; I bet it's plastic wrap!"

Sadie covers her mouth to hide her grin.

Ethan stops before us. "I am Ethan, the invincible. I goeth forth to playeth my game in peace."

He stalks over to a rock and plunks down, taking a drink from his water bottle.

"Is that a sock over the lid? Gross!" Sadie cries.

Ethan throws an answer over his shoulder. "It's keeping the bugs out!"

"It's a sock! A dirty one, I'm sure!"

"I rinsed it out first," he fires back.

It's all Sadie and I can do to keep from all-out laughing as he plays. I've almost got it under control when he groans and plops back on the rock, his "metal hat" dinging. "Seriously? A dead battery? After all that preparation?"

A shadow flashes by. *Splat.*

"I'm hit!" Ethan scrambles up, searching his torso. "Ha-ha, blue jay, you hit nothing but Saran Wrap! Wahoo! A point for Ethan!"

He carefully unwraps the plastic wrap and comes over, tucking his game into his pocket. "Any progress on the clue?"

"Nothing. Nada. Noodle," I say.

Ethan grunts, holding up his shield as the bird returns to her nest.

"Maybe it's time to give up on this one," he says.

"No pot of gold?" Sadie moans.

"I agree with Ethan. This one is too tough. There's no way we can figure it out," I say. "There's no telling what Mom and Dad will say. We need to stick together and agree it's impossible."

"Right," Sadie agrees.

"Ten-four, good buddy." Ethan salutes as Dad unzips the tent.

"Let's go," I say. That feeling is pulsing for no reason in my chest. It's never failed to warn me when danger is near, but I punch it down and take a deep breath.

"Dad, we've really enjoyed this treasure hunt, especially since it's here at the Grand Canyon. And, you know, we've been wondering about that pot of gold a lot. But the truth is, this clue is just too tough. We can't do it. There's just not enough to go on."

Sadie slips the fabric into my hand. I hold it up and shrug.

"We're going to have to quit."

Dad narrows his eyes. "What's that?"

"Umm...the clue."

"No, it isn't! Let me see it."

I hand it to him, my stomach in a knot. "What do you mean it's *not* our clue?"

"For one, I've never seen it in my life. And two…" But Dad falls silent as he fingers the dark stain at the bottom.

I whisper, "If this cloth didn't come from you, then what if somebody really needs help?"

Dad's serious gaze finds mine. "Where did you find this?"

"On the Shoshone Point Trail, right after you told me we'd missed it."

"And you took the left-hand trail, straight to the little rock outcropping?" Dad asks.

"Exactly, then One Paw dug this up and tried to steal it."

"One Paw?"

"The gray fox with one white paw," Sadie says.

"Honey!" Dad calls Mom from the tent.

"Good morning!" she says with a cheery smile, like always, but her expression disappears as she looks at us. "What's wrong?"

"Look at this! The kids thought it was their clue."

Mom's careful fingers trace the words *Help me*

as her brow knits. "Greg. Is this real? I mean, how can we even tell how old it is?" She bites her lip when she finds the dark stain. "This could be serious."

"The fabric still has a bright color. Look at my backpack. It's only a year old, but it's already fading from the sun," I offer.

"Good point." Dad nods, "Could it be some sick joke?"

Mom shakes her head. "I don't think so. This is dried blood, Greg."

Sadie gasps, covering her mouth, her eyes locked on the dark blotch.

"I think it's fresh because you can see where the rain hit the chalk, see?" I point to the faint dots in the white powder.

"You're right, and it hasn't rained for a month before the other night, so we can figure its age to be a month or less," Mom says.

"That's not a very short window of time," Dad says flatly.

"But look here," Ethan grabs the fabric and slaps it against his leg. There's a poof of chalk, and when he holds it up, the letters are much fainter.

"Ethan!" Mom scolds.

"Sorry, but you can see that it couldn't have gone through much wind or anything else because the chalk comes off very easily." His voice gets quieter as he goes.

"You do make a good observation there, Ethan." Dad's words soothe him. "But why do you have a trash-can lid strapped to your head? Never mind. We better get this message to a ranger right away."

That feeling coils outward into my arms. Someone is in trouble...*how can we ever find them in a place as massive as the Grand Canyon?*

-16-

"Maybe somebody lost his video game!" Ethan says as we drive away from the ranger station, where we left the clue. "That would be reason enough to write a note like that! If we find them, I'll let them play mine for five minutes. No, that would use too much battery. Maybe two minutes."

I sigh. "Dad, do you think the rangers will figure it out?" I can't get rid of the sour feeling in my stomach.

"Well, I'm sure they'll look into it, but to be honest, they don't seem convinced that we didn't make it up ourselves." Dad grips the wheel. "I think we should try to figure out this mystery ourselves."

"Me too!" Sadie says with relief.

"I sure wish One Paw could tell us where he found it," I mutter.

"Hey, you might have something there." Sadie snaps her fingers. "One Paw knows more about this than anyone else."

"He's a fox, Sadie," I say flatly. "He can't talk."

"Nope. But according to the animal tracking map I've been working on, I know he has daily habits. See here, he's near the rim every evening. But we sighted him deep in the canyon at midday. So maybe we could track him and find more clues."

"What a brilliant idea, Sadie!" Dad says. "I think we should try it."

"That means traveling on foot into the canyon in this serious heat. We're going to have to use all our training and smarts," Mom says, eyeing us carefully.

"We will."

"Let's pack twice as much water as we think we will need," Mom says.

"And binoculars!" Sadie is already headed toward the tents.

I refill my CamelBak water reservoir, then drink as much as I can through the straw and top it off again. I pull on a baseball cap and check my trusty bag. My basic first-aid kit is at the bottom, a Ferro rod and a pack of ashes and cotton balls for making fire rolls. A brand-new survival blanket only takes up as much space as a folded paper.

"Let's all bring extra T-shirts to drape over our heads and backs. We've got to beat this sun every way possible," Dad calls from the other tent. "Ethan, you can use another one of mine."

I tuck my largest T-shirt under my hat until it's comfortable, and it provides an extra layer of sun protection for my neck. I step out to find Mom slicing cucumbers from her camp cooler.

"Okay, Sadie, it's early morning. So where do we have the best chance of sighting One Paw?" Dad asks.

I see that Dad has a T-shirt tucked under his hat

the same as I do. It makes me happy inside to be so similar to him.

Sadie pulls out her animal map. I look at it, impressed with her work. She's mapped out the daily habits of blue jays, two foxes, two types of lizards, eight different squirrels, and one owl.

"So, One Paw is marked in purple. I have the time of day listed next to each sighting. My theory is One Paw is a daddy, and he's feeding kits."

"Kits?" Dad asks.

"That is what a baby fox is called."

"Sounds like a sandwich kit to me. Build your own salami, cheese, lettuce, and tomato!" Ethan rubs his belly.

"Pack extra food for Ethan," Mom mutters, returning to her cooler.

"Anyway, that's why he has been so bold about stealing food; it's for his babies. His den seems to be somewhere on the rim, and he spends the night there to guard it from predators. During the day he goes hunting for food."

"*Thieving*," Ethan interjects.

"It's all the same to him. Look here." She points to the purple dot on the Shoshone Point Trail. "He was coming up from deeper in the canyon when Ethan scared him and got the message. So, my theory holds true. He was trying to take the scrap back to his den."

"Some meal that would've been." Ethan crosses his arms.

"The best thing we can do is head to the South Kaibab Trailhead and start scouting for One Paw there," Dad says, tightening his belt.

Mom's mouth hangs open. "Are we really hiking the Grand Canyon on foot? Remember how tired we were when the mules did all the work?"

"I know it, Ruth. We'll take it slow and prepare ourselves. Somebody's hurt out there. Ethan's right about the chalk it was written with; it wouldn't have lasted long in the weather. We can't ignore this cry for help. The rangers have a full plate already and not enough proof that someone is lost in the park."

"Neither do we," Mom hesitates.

"We've got to try," Dad says.

"I'm ready. We'll be careful, Mom," I add.

"Ethan, you're going to have to give up the trash-can lid as a hat," Dad says.

Ethan studies the sky carefully. "Okay, but bird bombs are not easy to get out of your hair in a tiny sink."

By the time we reach the South Kaibab Trail-head, my fingers are tingling. *Lord, please help us find this person.* As I stare out over the rim, I'm shocked again by its size. *What chance do we have of finding one needle in this 18-mile-wide haystack?* I think we are all experiencing the same fear as we stand at the edge of the rim.

-17-

Ethan's hands are resting on his slim hips. "Nearly impossible odds, intense life-threatening heat, and one wily fox as a guide. What are we waiting for?" With that, he steps onto the tight set of switchbacks at the beginning of the descent.

"Yeah," Sadie says as she follows him. We search the layered rocks for the flitting shape of One Paw without success. I bite the straw from my pack and enjoy the cool water flowing. We hike down four steep switchbacks, and my leg muscles are burning from the effort. I wipe my brow where quick-drying sweat collects under my hat brim.

Something suddenly catches my eye. It's a pebble bouncing its way down the steep rock face. I turn back to concentrate on the trail. *Wait. What made the pebble fall?* I stop and study the red rocks shimmering in the heat.

"There!" I cry. Something is moving down the rock ledge right below the trail. "It's One Paw!" I point at his barely visible form. He is following the switchbacks on his own little trail that runs parallel to our own.

"It's him!" Sadie adds as she catches sight of his bright-white front paw.

"Okay, everybody, safety first," Dad warns. "The worst thing we could do is get hurt because we aren't paying attention."

"Oh, he's fast!" Mom groans as One Paw drops out of sight for a moment. We increase our pace, trying to stay ahead of the fox, but it doesn't last long. Soon he's worked his way well below us on the trail. He's now just a shadow in the heat waves. We press on for a long time, catching sight of One Paw far below us every few minutes.

Sadie groans, "We can't keep up! What are we going to do?"

"We're going to take a break," Mom says, producing a moan from the rest of us. "No, we take a five-minute break to eat and drink and then go on." Mom won't hear of anything else. I must admit it's a relief to sit down. The water in my CamelBak reservoir is warm now and not nearly as refreshing.

Ethan pulls out his game. "Yes! Level 52!"

I shake my head as Sadie pulls out her map. "I wonder if One Paw goes to Phantom Ranch every day?" She chews on her lower lip.

"It would be logical for him to do. I mean, it's one of the few places that has plant growth in the canyon, which means more mice and rats. Plus, people stop there with food. I would say he does," Dad says.

"Right, and at the pace he is holding, he'll probably be there in an hour or so."

I continue her thought. "He'll spend late morning there hunting."

"Thieving!" Ethan interjects with a smile, not even looking up from his game.

I roll my eyes. "When a certain member of our party was claimed by said fox it was noon, remember? So, he was already on his way up to the rim. If we keep hiking down and reach Indian Garden, we might see him there around lunchtime."

"That's a great plan, kids," Mom agrees. "Let's shoot for Indian Garden. With some shade and the good view there, we can keep watch for One Paw."

"Time to go," Dad says, dusting off his pants.

"YES!" Ethan shouts, throwing his hands high.

I gasp as time seems to slow down because Ethan's exuberant movement and sweaty hand causes him to lose his grip on his game. We watch it spinning through the extra-thin air for what seemed like a long time.

Dad leaps for Ethan, who's stretching for the game over the edge of the trail. Dad lands hard on Ethan's legs just as he loses his balance. "Whoa!" Ethan cries.

Mom's hand hits her chest. "Oh, thank God you didn't fall! Ethan, what were you thinking?"

"My game!" he groans. We all lean out carefully. The game is just a speck now, still falling. We hear a distant crinkling sound as it lands hard on a boulder below.

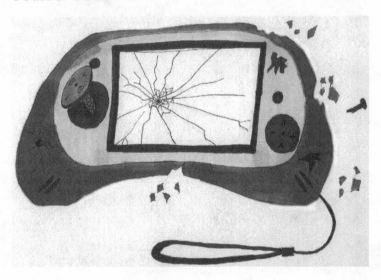

"Nooooo!" Ethan shouts.

"I, for one, am not sad that game is gone," Dad says, letting go of Ethan's legs after he's sure he's settled on the trail again.

"Uncle Greg, how could you say such a thing?"

"It's making you miss out on life. You were addicted to it, and that means you weren't controlling you; the game was. Anytime that happens, it's dangerous. You nearly jumped into the Grand Canyon after it."

"I could have caught it," he says with his arms crossed.

"And who would have caught you?" Mom asks, her voice pinched.

Ethan just shrugs.

"Well, let's head for the Indian Garden and hopefully find the fox who knows everything," Dad says, turning back to the trail.

"Just think," I say, "every step down means one we've got to take back up."

-18-

As Ethan sits on the same boulder at Indian Garden, he pulls out a fake game and moves his thumbs over nothing. Then he flops onto his back.

Sadie pats his arm. "It's okay, Ethan. I'm glad to have you back. Besides, you only told two jokes this trip. Not hearing your jokes has been weird."

"It's no time for joking; my game is gone."

She shrugs, then scans the trail ahead for movement. The mules trudge up the hill, and I pick Daisy out right away.

"Hey, girl!" I say, patting her nose after her rider dismounts. We search carefully for One Paw, willing him to show up like he did the last time.

"Come on, One Paw. You've got to lead us to the person who needs our help," I whisper. But the mule riders soon pack up and continue up the trail, leaving us alone in the quiet again.

Mom shields her eyes with one hand, studying the sky. I look up to see a wide funnel shape of buzzards circling down to a point.

"Those are California condors, Mom," Sadie exclaims. "I counted 12! How cool is that!"

"Yeah," Mom says in a voice that's not at all sure. She studies them for a long time. Dad puts an arm around her shoulder, but I still catch their whispers. "That doesn't bode well, does it?"

"No, but there's no way to know what they're after—probably a dead animal," Dad says without conviction.

"What if we never find the person?" Sadie asks

with tears in her eyes. Mom puts an arm around her as we sit in the narrow shade that's left. "We've done our best, honey. I can't think of anything else we can do."

As we sit in silence, the heat is like an oven, sucking the energy out of us. The mood of our entire troop plummets as the minutes tick past.

"All right," Dad sighs. "It's time to start back up."

"No!" Sadie and I say. Ethan just groans with his eyes shut.

"Come on, kids." Mom pulls us to our feet. With every step back up the South Kaibab Trail, I feel heavier, and the warning in my chest grows until I can barely stand it.

I turn, gazing back over the trail. "There he is!"

Everyone turns, but One Paw is long gone.

"Come on, I saw him. He's headed to the left. After him!" I shout, hurrying down the path.

"Isaiah, go careful and slow," Mom warns.

Ethan's long legs eat up the distance, so he's the first one to see around the ledge. "There!"

A bushy tail disappears behind another set of fallen rocks.

"Wait, we can't go everywhere that a fox can go. Being off the trail in the canyon can be deadly," Dad warns.

"Greg," Mom puts a hand on Dad's arm. "One Paw is headed straight for the condors." Her face is pale again.

"You're right. Kids, we've got to brace ourselves for the worst. One Paw could have found that note days after the person wrote it, and in this heat…"

Sadie covers her mouth with her hands, her eyes wide as she studies the descending condors. "We've got to hurry, then! I see One Paw."

The fox is cutting across a ledge piled with rocks fallen from above.

"He's making it look easy. I'll go first, no rushing. This is probably a bad idea."

"Dad, we can't give up," Sadie insists.

We set out after One Paw, picking out a surprisingly decent trail.

"Look, Mom!" Sadie points to a sandy area that's full of different boot prints that don't match dads. "Lots of people have been here before."

"You're right, Sadie," Dad says as he crouches, studying the way ahead. "This actually looks like a decently well-used trail."

The condors are nearly above us now and we press on, the sun searing as the heat wafts off the cliff to our left like an oven.

"Shh," Sadie spreads her hands, listening.

A sharp bark echoes ahead.

"What could that mean?" Ethan's brows knit, caught up now in our quest.

"Let's go find out," Dad says, spreading his arms and turning sideways to squeeze along an incredibly narrow section of the ledge.

"Okay," he says from the other side. "Take my hand as you come across."

I hold my breath when it's my turn. All I can picture is Ethan's game spinning in a free fall. My chest is pumping by the time I'm on Dad's side.

"Good job, son," he says.

Another yip draws us forward.

"What's that?" I ask, pointing at a bolt with a shiny round end screwed into the canyon wall.

"There's another one even higher!" Ethan says, pointing.

"This is a climbing wall!" Dad says. "That explains the trail too."

A condor swoops past, and the rush of air from his giant wings makes us all duck.

"Come on!" Dad pushes ahead until we reach a deep crevasse that's a few feet wide and hundreds of feet deep. A series of bolts curve up the nearly sheer cliff next to us.

"There's a section of rope up there!" Sadie whispers and she's right, a blue climbing rope draped through two bolts dangles, frayed at one end.

"Where's the guy who used that rope?" I whisper back, the strange feeling of the place pressing down on me. A soft whine draws our attention past the crevasse.

"One Paw!" Mom breathes.

The fox is facing off with a far-larger condor standing on a ragged boulder. One Paw darts forward, nipping at the condor's belly. The bird snaps back, but the fox is quicker.

"Mom!" Sadie's shout makes One Paw dart away, and the condor soars away. "A man is down there!"

I search where she's pointing, and sure enough, down in another deep crevasse is a climber wedged between the rocks.

"Is he…" Sadie looks green.

"He twitched!" Dad shouts. "He's not gone yet!"

A weak groan echoes up the sides of the chasm.

"How do we reach him?" Dad slams the cliff with his palm, finding no safe way down to the injured man. "If only we had some climbing gear!"

There's a motion behind us, and I turn just in time to see Ethan at a full sprint.

"NO!" Mom screams, but Ethan is already airborne over the crevasse, his arms flailing.

-19-

Mom sags against the cliff when he lands safely on the far side. "So help me, Ethan! Do not ever do that again!"

"Sorry, Aunt Ruth, but he needs help now. Toss me some water, will you?"

Sadie and I load two packets of blue electrolyte powder into a water bottle. I know how bad it will taste, but the climber will need it desperately.

I toss it over to Ethan, struggling against the dizzy feeling near the edge. Then Ethan carefully works his way down to the climber. The man's pack has been smashed nearly up over his head by his body weight jammed tightly into the cleft of the rock. The pack straps are so tight that his arms are swollen. He must have reached over his head and ripped the fabric from his pack.

"He won't drink!" Ethan's voice cracks.

"Take it easy, Ethan. You'll have to force his mouth open. Just wet his lips first. Don't give him too much at once; he could choke," Dad coaches.

Ethan makes a pained face as the man's head flops to one side; his right leg is jammed at an awful angle in the crevasse. The other leg is badly skinned and swollen.

"There, he swallowed some!" Ethan shouts excitedly.

"Here!" I dig frantically in my pack for my survival blanket. I toss it down to Ethan. "Make him a sun shelter with it."

"Good idea," Dad says, reaching into his pack.

"I'm going to go help him, Dad."

"No way. Ethan did that without permission."

"Sorry, Uncle Greg," Ethan says, still focusing on getting liquid into the climber.

"Now that there you're there safely, I'm glad, but don't you ever pull a stunt like that again."

"Yes, sir." Ethan switches to unfolding the survival blanket and spreading it over the area to create shade.

"Okay, everybody press back against the cliff. I'm going to shoot this." Dad holds up a short pistol.

"Where did you get that?" I ask.

"The ranger loaned it to me just in case we found this fellow. It's a flare gun, and they're watching for it. The smoke trail should lead the rescue team straight here."

We press against the cliff and plug our ears. Dad points it skyward. "Now, not to hit a critically endangered bird. Go!" He pulls the trigger and the bright-red flare spits and sputters high into the air. Its arrival breaks the quiet spiral of condors, and an oily scent of smoke fills the air. The thick line of smoke hangs lazily, pointing directly at us.

"His leg is still bleeding!" Ethan grimaces as he looks at it.

"I've got a first-aid kit!" I toss it down to Ethan, but he misses the catch, and the thin plastic box breaks open on the rocks.

"See the stretchy white band? Use it as a tourniquet on his leg."

We coach Ethan through patching up the man and getting more water into him. By the time he's slurped up two bottles, he rasps out his first words. "You came…"

"We found your note," Ethan replies. The man's face crumples, and I think he would be crying if his body had any extra water for tears.

"I fell two days ago. Fox has been here every day sitting with me or chasing off those awful birds." He groans in pain. "Fox took my note too."

"We call that fox One Paw, and he brought your note straight to us," Ethan says as he puts the third bottle to the man's cracked lips. Now that he's moved his head, I can see a deep bruise on his cheek as well.

"Ethan, catch!" I toss him a sheathed camping

knife. "Cut off his pack so his arms are free." Ethan has a time trying to slip the knife through the tight space between the straps and the man's skin.

"Where did you fall from?" Dad shouts down as the first strap pings free.

"Fourth bolt," the man rasps without looking up. We crane our necks, and my mouth falls open. The fourth bolt is high, really high.

"How did he survive?" Mom murmurs.

Voices echo, coming down the trail.

-20-

"Here, we're here!" I call.

The tension in my chest drains away as the rescue team approaches through the intense heat waves.

"Wow!" The lead ranger looks down at Ethan and the climber. "How did you find him?"

"A very special fox," Sadie answers.

"And a very special girl," Mom adds, hugging her close.

The team pulls on harnesses, and the climbers clip into the climbing bolts.

They climb over the edge of the crevasse and ascend, carefully turning the locks on their carabiners at each bolt. Minutes later they are working on the climber.

"What's your name?" the lead ranger asks.

"Sam Russell."

"Can you feel this?" The ranger gently pinches Sam's finger.

Sam groans, his eyelids fluttering. "No."

The ranger frowns, easing a brace on Sam's neck. The others unfold the stretcher and lock it open.

"Okay, let's lift him out."

Sadie buries her face in Mom's shirt as the men try to lift Sam out of the crevasse. They try over and over, changing grip, but Sam's leg is jammed deep in the rocks.

"It's no good; his leg has swelled up in there." The rangers are sweating, balancing on the ledge.

"Wait," Mom cries, digging through her pack. "I've got some tanning oil. If you pour it down his leg, maybe it might help his leg slip out." Mom tosses it gently.

"It's worth a try." As the ranger fumbles with

the oil, it bounces once on the deep-red rocks and spins toward the canyon.

"No!" Ethan's arm sweeps out, catching it right before it goes over.

"Nice move, kid. You did some good first aid here too. Especially the sun shield. Sam sure doesn't need any more sunshine." The man pours the entire bottle of oil along Sam's leg. "One more try, team. We don't have much time."

At first, I wonder what he means, then Sadie's face peeks out, "I hear the helicopter."

I turn, scanning the sky. "There it is!"

"Heave, altogether!" The team strains, and Sam groans in pain.

"Kid, grab his climbing harness and pull."

Ethan's face goes white. "Okay." He grabs the big ring and pulls until the veins on his neck stand out. "Here…he…comes!" Ethan says through gritted teeth. Sam's leg finally slips loose, and the rangers settle him onto the stretcher.

The *wump-wump* of the helicopter pounds in

my chest. The rangers strap down Sam, then clip a stiff cover over him.

"Everybody, get back against the wall! The prop wash is going to be brutal," the ranger shouts over the oncoming bird.

My hair flies straight up, then sand, and rocks sting my legs. The helicopter tips toward us so close I can see the pilot chewing gum. A paramedic in the back slides open a wide door and carefully drops a cable toward the rangers.

Then the wind rises, and I cover my face as Dad's strong arms press us against the cliff. The wind pummels us, and I can hardly breathe in the hot, stinging sandstorm. It seems like an eternity till the helicopter glides away.

I blink rapidly to clear my eyes full of grit, and I catch sight of Sam on his stretcher, swinging a mile high over the grandest canyon in the world. The ranger pats Ethan on his back, raising a cloud of dust.

"You did good, kid! Now let's get you back up

to your family." The ranger lets Ethan, who's still holding the climber's pack, use his harness to climb back to us.

When we're all together, the ranger says, "Well, that was one lucky climber. How did you find him, anyway?"

"A fox with one white paw brought us his note, then we tracked the fox here," Sadie says happily.

"Ha! I know that rascal. He stole my lunch last week. But he's got a den with five pups to feed way up on the rim, so I didn't mind too much."

"I knew it!" Sadie says.

-21-

We pick our way out to the main trail, and the rangers spread out to talk to folks who are hiking into the canyon.

"Excuse me, sir. How far are you planning to hike today?" I hear one of them ask.

"Well, I figured I would go till I get tired, then I'll turn around."

"Okay, you might want to rethink that. Remember, the canyon is a mountain in reverse. The hard part is getting back out. By the time you're tired, you're too far from the rim to make it."

"Come on, crew," Dad says, "Let's start our own ascent."

I groan after we climb only one switchback. "The rangers are right; the rim seems as hard to reach as the moon." I pant in the heat. "Mom, do you think Sam is going to be okay?"

Mom stops and makes us all look at her in the eyes. "He is a lot better off now than he was when he was stuck on the cliff. And we would never have found him without Sadie's animal smarts."

"Okay, let's take a break here; there's a small overhang with some shade." Dad leads us to a low-hanging ledge just off the trail. He ducks low and searches inside. "No snakes, so let's use it."

We crawl into the shade, sitting cross-legged; we're now completely out of the burning sun.

"Ah." Ethan leans his head back. "That was quite an experience." He pulls Sam's shredded pack onto his lap. "How will we get this back to Sam?"

"We'll find a way later. The rangers can probably handle returning that to him. You know, now that I think about it, Sam passed us while we were on the mules," Dad says.

"You're right, Dad! He told that lady that the Egyptian stuff was a hoax," I say.

"Yeah, and she finally stopped talking about it!" Ethan adds.

"We should have remembered the strange color of his pack," Sadie says, shaking her head.

"It wouldn't have helped us find him, though. Hey, speaking of the Egyptian hoax…" Dad juts out his chin, looking at a long string of people hiking behind the man the rangers had told to stop selling his merchandise at the park.

"Almost there, everyone. A few more moments, and you will see the Egyptian artifacts for yourselves!" he announces, pointing past our hideout.

"Oh, look, there *is* a path that passes here." Ethan points to a faint trail running below us.

"Let's take a breather and get some water; everybody, tighten your shoelaces. We're stepping off the trail to find Kincaid's Cave," Mr. Sanders says.

"What?" Mom whispers. "I looked up everything I could on Kincaid's Cave, and the experts say its location is at Lake Powell above the Glen Canyon Dam."

"Things are getting fishier all the time. Anybody for clearing up one more mystery today?" Dad asks.

"Yes!" we whisper back.

"Then we've got to get to this so-called Kincaid's cave before they do. Go quiet and stick together." Dad nods once, then crawls farther down past an outcropping, easing out onto the tight trail out of the sight of Mr. Sanders and his group.

-22-

We tiptoe forward, and sure enough, we see a dark cave opening straight ahead. I pull out my flashlight and shine it inside. A chain is blocking off one section of wall.

The cave is bigger than I thought it would be, and the air, although dry, gets deliciously cooler every step we take. I squint at the area the chain is keeping us from. Strange markings are written in vertical rows.

"Hieroglyphics," Dad whispers, clicking on another light.

Ethan slips under the chain and pushes his finger into the rock. Sadie gasps, Ethan's fingers sink easily into the area with the ancient Egyptian writing. "Fake hieroglyphics! This wall has been smeared with clay."

Ethan does a sad job of smoothing out his handprint, and we move farther into the cave. More chains surround an area strewn with painted clay pots and some golden dishes.

Sadie slips under the chain this time, turning one plate over. "Made in China? This is no ancient artifact!"

We huddle together, our eyes wide as we shuffle into a deeper part of the cave.

"It's…a…a…" Ethan's finger trembles as he points straight ahead. "…mummy!"

Even with all the fakes behind us, we have a creepy sense that this mummy is real.

Dad snorts, "I highly doubt that." He stoops under the chain and slips behind the life-size mummy. Soon Dad's eyes are peeking through the wrapping.

"*Ooooohhhhhoooo!*" Dad says in a scary voice.

Ethan nearly jumps into Mom's arms.

"It's fake—just like the rest," Dad says, stepping out again. "It's only a light plastic shell with gauze wrapped around it."

Ethan steps away from Mom, crossing his arms. "I knew that."

I roll my eyes. "Sure you did. Dad, what's going on here?"

"I have a feeling Mr. Sanders has charged the group he's leading here a pretty penny for the privilege of seeing his fakes. Hey, let's hide, and I'll see if I can step out and get some information from someone in the crowd."

We scatter because voices are echoing down the dry rock walls. I dive behind a huge plastic urn that's painted with golden hieroglyphics.

I click off my light and try to still my heaving chest. Sadie is crouched behind a set of child-sized mummies I hadn't noticed before, and Ethan slips behind the main mummy, his bright blue eyes now peeking through the eye lots.

I hold my breath as Mr. Sanders steps into our cavern with a flaming torch held high. "Behold, the main chamber!" his voice echoes.

The people huddle in tight groups, gasping when they see the mummy. Dad slips from the deep shadows, making two men nearly jump out of their skin.

"Sorry," he says softly. "I didn't mean to scare you. Say, did you pay $50 for this tour?"

"Fifty dollars?" one man says. "It was $200! But look at all of this; I can't believe it's real. And I'm even seeing it with my own eyes."

Dad rubs his chin. "Huh."

"Silence, please!" Mr. Sanders calls. "We are now in the presence of King Taharqa, the last in the royal lineage of ancient rulers!" He reverently leads the group back to the chain protecting the plastic mummy while I correct him in my mind. It's not a *king*; it's called a *pharaoh!*

"Ugh...*argh!*"

I blink hard at Pharaoh Taharqa. He seems to

tremble. A nervous twitter comes from the crowd. The mummy jerks hard. *"Ooooohhhh!"*

I cover my mouth to keep from shouting at Ethan. What on earth is he thinking?

"Ah, ah, AH!" the mummy shouts, skittering forward toward the crowd. They scream, the sound like a freight engine in the cave. People scramble for the entrance, pushing and elbowing to get out first. Mr. Sanders stands frozen before the mummy with his eyes wide.

"Bahhllt!" Pharaoh Taharqa growls. Mr. Sanders drops his torch and sprints for the entrance, screaming. "Wait for me!"

Dad is the only one left standing in the middle. A heartbeat later, Ethan's normal voice reaches me. "Got him."

"Ethan, what possessed you to do such a thing?" Dad asks, as the rest of us step out.

"There was a tarantula in there, and he climbed into my hair! But I got him," Ethan says, still sweeping his hands through his hair.

"Did you see their faces?" Mom giggles, and her laughter infects the rest of us.

"Well, I think that's the last time Mr. Sanders will try that trick," Dad affirms. "Still, I'll be sure to let the rangers know when we return Sam's pack."

"Yeah, he was as white as a sheet!" I laugh, remembering his expression.

"Let's get back to the rim," Mom says, picking up Sam's shredded pack.

"Aww, but the cave is so cool," Sadie whines.

"That's true, but you are all super behind on your clues! We've got one day left here, and you haven't found your pot of gold yet," Mom says.

"Oh, I forgot about our clues! I guess we really missed the one at Shoshone Point, didn't we?" I shine my light ahead as we walk through the cave.

"Yes, you entirely missed it, but you found something infinitely more important. At least Sam Russell would say so!" Dad adds. "Tomorrow, we will go back to Shoshone Point and see what you find."

"Yes!" Sadie pumps her fist in the air.

"As long as One Paw didn't steal our clue," Ethan gripes.

"No worries about that," Dad says easily, making me wonder just what sort of clue it could be.

Sam's pack swings from Mom's shoulder, his climbing gear dangling right before me. "Hey, isn't this carabiner supposed to have a lock on it?" I point at one of his carabiners. "You know…the part that twists over the hinge to lock it closed?"

Dad stops and studies Sam's equipment in the beam of my light. "You're right, Isaiah, and look at this." He holds up a bent carabiner with the frayed end of blue rope clipped to it. "This might have been what gave out when Sam fell. It's strange though; climbers are usually super careful to check their equipment."

-23-

"Okay. Off you go after your clue," Dad says at the small trail that cuts off from the Shoshone Point Trail.

Sadie giggles and takes off running. Ethan and I jog after her. "What do you think it could possibly be?" Ethan pants.

"Could be anything," I respond.

We come up on Sadie, standing with her hands on her hips. "There's nothing here," she declares.

"Oh, boy," I say because she's right. After a careful search, we plunk down in the center of the clearing.

"Do you think your dad will help us?"

"Nope," I say.

"Hey, what does a cloud wear under his rain-coat?"

"What?"

"Thunder-wear!" Ethan laughs at his joke.

I nod. "Having you back is sure nice, Ethan."

"Yeah. I guess you guys were right. *Road Tron* was sort of my whole life for a little while."

"Why did you start playing video games, any-way?" Sadie asks, tossing pebbles at a bigger rock.

"I was so bored. I mean, when we're not on a trip, and I'm just at home, well, there's not much to do. Playing video games seemed like a great way to pass some time. But then, playing the game got to be all I wanted to do."

"*All things in moderation* is what Mom always says," I add.

"Yeah, I guess if I had kept it as a sometimes thing, it wouldn't have been so bad. But it's official."

"What is?" I ask.

"I'm not going to play anymore. Thanks to the

blue jays and all of you, I believe I have learned my lesson."

"And your game falling into the abyss of the Grand Canyon had nothing to do with it?" Sadie asks.

"Well, there was that, too. Hey, two pickles fell out of a jar; what did one say to the other?"

"Ouch?" Sadie's nose wrinkles up on one side.

"No, dill with it!"

"Ha-ha. That one was actually funny. But what about this clue?" I frown.

"Wait. I think we're sitting in it." Sadie goes still.

"Look all around. See the rocks of similar size in a big circle?"

I twist to follow her pointer finger.

"Dad wasn't worried about One Paw ruining his clue because it was set in stone!"

We stand up and scout farther. "I think you're right, Sadie! These are giant letters, and we were sitting inside of an A."

"Let's climb up a little higher to see it better."

Sadie is already scaling an outcropping.

We ease over the rock ledge and look down.

"It says *Skywalk!*" Ethan points.

"But what does that mean?" I wonder.

"I've seen that word somewhere! I have a brochure about a skywalk; I need my pack."

We climb down, and Sadie pulls out a glossy sheet with "Walk on the Sky" printed at the top.

"Wow! The skywalk is a glass-floored walkway built over the edge of the western rim of the canyon."

"You can see a mile straight down beneath your feet." Sadie does a little dance. "This will be an amazing ending to our trip."

We race back to Mom and Dad who are sitting and laughing as they catch sight of us rushing toward them.

"Well?" Dad asks.

"It's the skywalk!" we shout.

"Yes!" Mom grins. "Let's go break camp, and we'll do the skywalk on our drive out."

"Oh, breaking camp. That's so sad," Sadie says.

"I agree." My hands are in my pockets, fidgeting at the thought.

Mom adds, "I know, but we've got to get back to real life sometime. Besides school starts in a few weeks." We all groan at that thought.

"But can you believe we saw five national parks in one year? It's been amazing. Which one was your favorite?" Mom asks.

"All of them!" Sadie shouts, making us all laugh.

"I concur," Ethan says.

"Each one has its own kind of specialness," I add.

By the time we're done packing, we still haven't seen Nate. I shove the last box into the truck. "I sure wish we could have said goodbye," I say, eyeing Nate's silent tent.

"Everybody in," Dad calls, and we settle in the truck.

Mom says, "It should take a few hours to get there. The western rim is quite a distance."

The wind kicks dust to form little whirlwinds as

we pull out of Desert View Campground. By the time we reach the western rim, I think Ethan has told us every joke he knows.

We get out and walk past a huge sign that reads "The Skywalk at Eagle Point."

Dad reads from the brochure: "The horseshoe-shaped bridge extends over 70 feet with nothing below, except the canyon for over 4000 feet down. Don't worry, though, the skywalk can withstand an 8.0 earthquake and sustained gusts of wind of over 100 mph! It's so strong, you could park 71 Boeing 747 airplanes on it—if they could all fit at one time. Let's do it!"

The building is nice and cool, and we each get a pair of white fabric booties to pull over our shoes to protect the glass floor of the skywalk.

"Please place all belongings in the locker you have been assigned. Empty your pockets of everything, including your phones. Not only could a dropped phone damage the glass, but we cannot risk littering in the canyon." An attendant repeatedly gives her instructions to the tourists who want to walk out on the skywalk.

After we've got our booties on and our pockets empty, we stride toward the glass floor of the bridge. The outside edges of the floor near the railings are painted brown and they look solid, but the center strip is clear. People step from the brown part onto the clear and freeze with their arms spread wide.

Inwardly, I snicker at their reaction, then I step onto the glass, and all my muscles seize up. Nothing is below me—not for a mile. My arms seem stuck with my elbows pointing out.

-24-

"Isa…" I hear Mom start to call my name, then I feel her gentle hand clasp my arm as she draws me back to the brown strip. "Did you get stuck?" She smiles at me.

"I didn't think I would!"

We all take turns "freezing" upon stepping onto the glass and rescuing each other. By the time we reach the farthest section, I'm able to take a few steps on my own. We laugh and beat our fears, and when we reach the far end of the bridge, we all link arms and bravely stride over the clear glass back into the building.

"Now I know what it feels like to fly," Sadie says

as we throw out the white booties, grab our stuff from our locker, and head back to the truck.

"Miss! Excuse me, Miss!"

We reach the truck, but the voice comes closer.

"Miss, you forgot these in your locker!"

I turn to see an attendant running toward us.

Sadie points at herself. "Me?"

"Yes!" The lady pants, trying to catch her breath as she hands Sadie some papers.

"No, these aren't…" Sadie says, then I catch sight of two more strangely shaped postcards. "Oh…" Sadie laughs. "Never mind; they are mine."

"Okay, Mom and Dad, what's up with all of these?" She holds them out, the new ones say, "blank and blank."

"Let me show you," Mom says, reaching into the truck. She pulls out a long picture frame that's painted gold with five blank spots for pictures. The first one is heart shaped.

"Wyoming goes there!" Sadie cries, pulling them from her notebook.

"Then Maine!" I snap the star-shaped postcard into its place.

"I still don't get it," Ethan says. Mom grins at Dad. "Greg, you tell them."

"What?" Sadie squeals.

"This year we camped in five national parks. Your mom and I have decided to do something crazy. We plan to visit five more next year! What do you think about that?"

"What?" I ask, feeling as if I could float away.

"Five new parks. Can you tell us which ones they'll be?" Mom looks at the full frame.

"Yellowstone?" I say, my voice filled with wonder at the thought of visiting there.

"Yes!" Mom grins.

"Maine? What's in Maine?" Sadie asks.

"Acadia!" Ethan says. "That park is an island!"

"California…" I snap my fingers, trying to make the name come. "Yosemite!"

"Bingo!" Mom cries.

The next one is easy; it's right next to Kentucky

where we live. "Indiana Dunes National Park!" Sadie cries as she points to the Indiana postcard.

"One more…" Mom coaches.

"Montana?" We're all stumped on that one.

"Glacier National Park!" Dad finally has mercy on us.

"*Wahoo!*" I shout, leaping high. "Five more parks and five more camping trips!"

"Five more Junior Ranger badges to earn!" Sadie squeals.

"Can I come?" Ethan begs.

Mom pulls him into a hug. "Of course, Ethan! What would a trip be without you?"

"Um…boring?" Ethan asks.

"Precisely!" Mom laughs.

We climb into the truck on cloud nine, and I reach for my trusty backpack, but it isn't where it should be at my feet.

"Oh, no! Mom, I left my bag at Desert View!"

She pulls down her sunglasses and turns to me. "You're kidding."

"NO!"

She sighs. "Well, we'll have to go back for it. It's a long way extra."

I clutch my hands together between my knees. "You think it will still be there?"

"It should be. We've only been gone a few hours," Dad says as he turns the truck in that direction.

The whole way, I worry about it. The first time I'd used it was at Grand Tetons when Kota, the black wolf, had taught me so much. Then the bear had clawed it in the Smokies. Plus, it's got all my Junior Ranger badges on it!

We pull into Desert View after what seems like an age, and I press my nose against the window. "There it is!" I shout as I slump in relief.

"What happened here?" Mom asks. Tents are strewn everywhere, and a lonely sock is tumbling down the road amid fallen branches.

"The wind must have gotten terrible. They say the canyon is so big, each section can have its own weather system," Dad says, pulling into our old site.

I jump out and grab my pack, hugging it close, while Sadie makes sure the jays' nest is still secure.

"It's fine. Oh, no!" Sadie points to a jumble of fabric and broken tent pegs. "That's Nate's tent!"

"Come on, we'll help him clean up. Then we've got to get going," Dad says.

We find Nate staring at the wreckage of his tent.

"Here, Nate," Ethan says softly. "We'll help you."

"What? Oh, thanks," he says glumly.

Dad and I return the tent to some form of its previous shape, while Ethan chases down the items that had fallen out of Nate's tumbling backpack. I'm thankful my pack has been tucked behind a boulder.

"That wind came up so fast," Nate mutters.

"Umm…" Ethan grabs Dad's elbow, quietly pulling him aside. "Uncle Greg, look what I found in Nate's stuff." He opens his hand to show us a lime-green carabiner lock and a small, serrated camp knife with fibers of blue rope clinging to it.

I gasp. Dad frowns, taking them from Ethan.

Then he strides up to Nate and says, "Would you like to explain these, Nate?"

Nate's face gets white as a sheet, and he groans, "Ho...How did you find those?"

"So, you don't deny that you shouldn't have them?" Dad presses.

I bite my lip, recalling Nate's reaction when he saw the clue made from Sam's lime-green pack. He'd taken off running after he saw it because he knew more about it than he let on.

An old beat-up pickup truck rattles to the site. Mr. Sanders gets out. "Nate, we've got to leave a day early. Say, what's going on here?"

Ethan and I stare open-mouthed at Mr. Sanders. Suddenly everything makes sense—the way Nate was left alone at the campsite, the boys making fun of him, and his reaction to Sam Russell, who said he had proof that Nate's dad was wrong about the Egyptian artifacts.

"Nate?" my dad says in his serious voice.

"I...I never meant to hurt him! *Honest*. I was

just so tired of him picking on my dad. Sam left all his gear sitting right there. I thought…" Nate starts to cry. "I thought I would just teach him a lesson that I could mess with him the same way he was ruining my dad's business."

"Some business…" Ethan mutters.

"Not anymore," Mr. Sanders sighs. "Everything fell apart. Nate, what you did was wrong. I know Sam has been a thorn in our side, but I'm going to have to call the authorities about what you did."

I bite my lip as I watch Nate crumple to the ground. And I wonder what I would've done in his situation. I believe that he really didn't think Sam would get hurt. But all the same, what Nate had done almost cost Sam his life.

Mr. Sanders calls the rangers himself. They pull in moments later. The entire story spills out of Nate with more tears.

The ranger nods. "At our last report, Sam is stable with a broken leg and some major bruising. So, you're not facing…more serious charges."

I'm relieved for Sam; he's going to make it. I'm so thankful we answered the cry for help.

"Sir, we've got a long journey ahead of us today. Are we free to go?" Dad asks, handing him the carabiner lock and knife.

"Yes, Mr. Rawlings. Have a safe journey home. Thanks for visiting the park."

-25-

We get into the truck, and I clutch my pack. "What's going to happen to Nate?" I ask.

Mom frowns. "Remember, every action you make has consequences. Some consequences are good, but sometimes they can be bad—even terrible. I feel awful for Nate. He was getting picked on because of his dad's lies. And that was something he couldn't change. Plus, he was alone all the time. What he chose to do doesn't make what he did okay, only sadder."

"A lot will depend on whether Sam Russell decides to press the issue. I really don't think Nate meant to hurt Sam; he just wanted to cause him some trouble. But the trouble he started was quickly out of control," Dad says.

"Just like my game...I didn't mean to get so stuck to it, but it ended up that way," Ethan adds.

"So make sure that everything you do is honest and true—no matter what the cost is to you. That means thinking everything through before you start something," Mom adds.

"Like the way you guys thought through us going to five more parks next year?" Sadie asks.

"Yes, we certainly spent some time thinking, planning, and calculating."

"What I want to know is, how did Dad plant all those clues without us seeing him?" I squint at him as he drives.

"Never underestimate the covert abilities of your father," Dad says with a smirk.

Sadie elbows me in the ribs with a sly grin. "Hey, Isaiah, are you gonna eat that sub?"

"Ugh!" I groan as she bursts out laughing.

Watch for more of
The Campground Kids
adventures
at www.bakkenbooks.com